"**Did I mention how beautiful you look in the morning?**" Mitch asked, tenderly brushing a bunch of curls back away from her face.

Hillary tried to gather all the wild curls into a fist. It was a hopeless job. Without half a can of mousse her hair looked like something out of *The Twilight Zone*. "My eyes get puffy and red when I cry."

"Don't cry." He lightly traced the freckles dancing across her cheekbones. "Is this where the angels kissed you?"

She rubbed at the offending marks that had caused her hours of misery during her youth. "I thought you were a man of science."

"I am. I know freckles are a small precipitation of pigment often brought out by the sun." He brushed his lips over the marks. "On you I could believe the angels really did kiss you and left behind their marks."

If he kept giving her such sweet compliments, she might even begin to appreciate the fact that Mother Nature had seen fit to bless her with deranged hair. "You, sir, are a dangerous man."

Mitch smiled and pulled her close. "I aim to please. . . ."

WHAT ARE *LOVESWEPT* ROMANCES?

They are stories of true romance and touching emotion. We believe those two very important ingredients are constants in our highly sensual and very believable stories in the *LOVESWEPT* line. Our goal is to give you, the reader, stories of consistently high quality that may sometimes make you laugh, sometimes make you cry, but are always fresh and creative and contain many delightful surprises within their pages.

Most romance fans read an enormous number of books. Those they truly love, they keep. Others may be traded with friends and soon forgotten. We hope that each *LOVESWEPT* romance will be a treasure—a "keeper." We will always try to publish

LOVE STORIES YOU'LL NEVER FORGET
BY AUTHORS YOU'LL ALWAYS REMEMBER

The Editors

Loveswept® 597

Marcia Evanick
Over the Rainbow

BANTAM BOOKS
NEW YORK · TORONTO · LONDON · SYDNEY · AUCKLAND

OVER THE RAINBOW

A Bantam Book / February 1993

*If you would be interested in receiving protective vinyl
covers for your Loveswept books, please write to this address
for information:*

*Loveswept
Bantam Books
P.O. Box 985
Hicksville, NY 11802*

ISBN 0-553-44364-X

Published simultaneously in the United States and Canada

*Bantam Books are published by Bantam Books, a division of
Bantam Doubleday Dell Publishing Group, Inc. Its trademark,
consisting of the words "Bantam Books" and the portrayal of
a rooster, is Registered in U.S. Patent and Trademark Office
and in other countries. Marca Registrada. Bantam Books, 666
Fifth Avenue, New York, New York 10103.*

PRINTED IN THE UNITED STATES OF AMERICA

OPM   0 9 8 7 6 5 4 3 2 1

To my newest bundle of joy,
Savannah Leigh.
Welcome to the world.
Love,
Mom

Prologue

"Miss Walker is the one."

Staring at Ethan, Callie Ferguson asked, "Are you sure?"

"Positive!" He looked down at the crumpled paper in his hand. "Number six says she has to like loud music. You told me she listens to music all the time."

"That's what she told me." Callie wished for the thousandth time that she could read the list Ethan held. The most important decision in her life was being made based on that list, and she couldn't even check for herself what was written there. It wasn't that she didn't trust her older brother, but he had been known to lie to her in the past. Like the time when she was three and he put her in a cardboard box and pushed her down the stairs. It hadn't been like a roller-coaster ride at all.

"You said she didn't scream when Johnny's frog

got loose in your class." Ethan pointed to number 5 on the paper.

Callie looked at the sentence and frowned. Being seven years old, she could read only every third word. "What does it say again?"

"She has to like snakes and other icky animals."

Ethan stared at his sister. From the expression on her face, it seemed she was going to back down. Sometimes girls were such sissies. Well, he wasn't going to let her turn sissy in this case. With the wisdom acquired from his nine years of living, he knew that Callie was going to have to be the bait. It wouldn't work any other way. "What's the matter, Callie? You like Miss Walker, don't you?"

"Yes."

"You're the one who said she'd be neat."

Callie hunched her shoulders and stared around their front yard. It was filled with dried leaves, and no one had bothered to take down the scarecrow from Halloween yet. Three lopsided jack-o'-lanterns were turning to mush on the porch, and dead brown flowers still overflowed the flower beds surrounding their house. Living in Maryland was sure different from living in Chicago. "Will Dad get mad at me?"

Ethan smiled and moved closer to her. "Dad never gets mad at you."

"That's because I never done nothing bad before."

"This ain't bad, Callie." Ethan carefully folded the piece of paper that listed the top ten things kids looked for in a mom and slipped it into the back pocket of his jeans. "Dad's probably going to buy you a brand-new bike for all your help."

"Really?"

"Sure. Once he meets Miss Walker and sees what a perfect mom she'd make for us."

"Do you think he'd get me the purple one in Gerhart's store window?"

"Yeah, and I bet they'll be married before Christmas and we can be a real family."

"But Dad says we don't need a mother, we have Eunice."

"She's a housekeeper, it's not the same thing. She can't be your homeroom mom, can she?"

"She said that a room full of seven-year-olds would make her break out in hives."

"See? She's too old to be a mom."

Callie followed Ethan to where they had left their bikes. "What about Aunt Ronnie?"

"She's Dad's sister, so she doesn't count. All kids have aunts—what we need is a mother."

"Do you really think they'll get married?"

Ethan hopped on his bike and waited for Callie. "Sure. All you have to do is what I told you to do, and by Christmas we'll have a real mother."

One

Mitch Ferguson glanced at his watch and muttered a curse. He was late for his meeting with his daughter's speech teacher, Miss Walker. When she had called yesterday to set up this appointment, she'd said that lately Callie was having trouble with her pronunciation and had hinted that perhaps some type of pressure, possibly from home, was the cause. The idea of his sweet, lovable daughter having problems was absurd. Callie was a well-adjusted and self-assured child. Miss Walker was probably mistaken, but he wasn't taking any chances. Callie and her brother, Ethan, were the center of his life.

He pulled open the door to the elementary school and hurried down the hall. Monstrous orange-paper pumpkins covered the walls, and witches riding brooms dangled from the ceilings. Halloween was still in evidence throughout the hall, but Thanksgiving was making its upcoming presence known by the seven-foot turkey outside the principal's office. Obviously every student was to make a feather to adorn the bird. It was a real shame that so far not every class had added its handiwork to the turkey. The gigantic bird looked plucked and ready for the oven.

He continued past the turkey and counted down three doors on the right. The wooden door was partly open, and a green sign on it proudly declared that this was MISS WALKER'S ROOM.

He took a deep breath and ran his fingers through his wind-tossed hair. His fingers froze halfway through their task as he glanced into the room. Miniature chairs faded from view as his eyes locked on a pair of black high heels. His gaze slowly inventoried the trim ankles, delectable calves, and sexy knees covered in sheer black stockings. The door blocked the rest of the tantalizing view. His gaze leisurely traveled back down the pair of legs to pause on the tiny black flower stitched into the stockings an inch above the slim ankle.

The first stirrings of desire shocked him out of his contemplation. Desire had no business rearing its head in his life, let alone at an elementary school. He had two children to raise, a sister to worry about, an eccentric housekeeper, and his career was starting down a different path. He ran his fingers through his hair again and took another deep breath. If the mere sight of a pair of legs could raise his blood pressure, maybe his sister was right. Maybe he had been out of circulation too long. With a last look at the intriguing ankle he raised his hand and knocked on the door. Disappointment shot through him as the legs disappeared from view accompanied by the sound of a chair scraping the tiled floor.

Hillary Walker put down the lesson plan she'd been writing as the loud knock vibrated through the classroom. Callie Ferguson's father had finally deemed it fit to keep his appointment. He was twenty minutes late. She stood up, brushed down her black wool skirt, and straightened the collar of her apple-green blazer. Then she checked to make sure the knot she had twisted all her hair up into that morning was still holding as she walked to the door. The sight of the man standing there caused her footsteps to falter. Callie's father wasn't what she expected.

He was wearing a well-worn brown leather jacket and jeans instead of a suit. Had she misunderstood Callie when she said her dad was a chemist? Mitchell Ferguson didn't look like any chemist she had ever run across. Where was the white lab coat, the plastic pen protector, and the thick glasses? Callie's father's dark brown hair was tousled and cried out to be combed. Her fingers itched to do the chore. His features had to have been sculpted by Aphrodite herself, and his dark eyes sparkled with intelligence and sensuality. The combination was a heady mixture for any female under the age of sixty. She cleared her throat with a rough cough before she asked, "Mr. Ferguson?"

Mitch looked farther into the room for another person. This couldn't be Callie's speech teacher. Teachers weren't built to look like this. The enticing legs were connected to a very alluring body trying desperately to hide under a proper skirt, blouse, and jacket. What looked like wild auburn hair was pulled back into a tight bun, and a small dusting of freckles were showing through her attempted cover-up of powder. Eyes the color of the first leaves of spring shone with friendly warmth and lips made to drive a man insane were smiling up at him. If this was the school's speech pathologist, he was going to start talking like Elmer Fudd and demand private sessions. "That's me, but who are you?"

Hillary raised a delicate eyebrow and glanced at the sign tacked to her door. She was definitely in the right room, and he did acknowledge he was the father she had a meeting with, so who did he think she was, the custodian? "Who would you like me to be?"

The woman I wake up next to tomorrow morning. Mitch slowly shook his head to clear the sensual haze. What in the hell was happening to him? he thought as he held out his hand. "Sorry, you must be Miss Walker." The voice gave her away. It was the same precise voice she used yesterday on the phone, even if it contained a slight undercurrent of laughter this afternoon.

Hillary quickly shook the outstretched hand. The less contact she had with Callie's gorgeous father, the better for her suddenly overactive hormones. It was considered in poor taste to drool over a student's father. She turned and walked back into the room. "Won't you come in?"

Mitch watched the enticing sway of the proper black skirt and swallowed hard, then followed her to a small round table and took the chair opposite her.

Her fingers visibly shook as she opened the folder lying on the table. The woodsy scent of his after-shave was playing havoc with her senses. "Mr. Ferguson, have you noticed any change in Callie this past week?"

He looked into her sincere eyes and sighed. She was serious. She really thought his daughter was having problems at home. Why was the whole world under the mistaken opinion that a man couldn't raise his own children without the help of a wife?

He unzipped his coat and shrugged it off. It looked as though he was in for a long haul convincing Hillary that Callie's home life was just fine. "The only change in Callie this past week was she lost another tooth that cost the Tooth Fairy a quarter and a pack of sugar-free gum."

Hillary smiled at the picture of Mitchell Ferguson playing Tooth Fairy for his seven-year-old daughter. "I know about the tooth, and it's not responsible for the deterioration in Callie's speech."

"What are you talking about?"

Confused, Hillary asked, "You haven't noticed a marked decline in the way Callie's been pronouncing her words?"

Mitch sputtered with indignation. "She's only seven years old and can't pronounce her *R*s sometimes. I didn't realize this school demands perfection from its students."

Hillary bristled at the accusation but fought for

calm. "Let me get this straight. You haven't noticed any changes in Callie's articulation?"

"None."

Hillary nervously picked up a pen and tapped it against the papers stacked in Callie's folder. She really hated to ask the next question but knew she must. Something was definitely wrong here. "May I ask a personal question?"

He leaned back in the chair and crossed his arms. "Sure."

"Have you talked to Callie at all this week?" His astonished brown eyes stared at her. "I mean besides the normal 'good morning' and 'good night' routine? Have you actually sat down and listened to her?"

He jumped to his feet. "That does it!" He placed both his hands on the table land leaned close to her. "Every time my daughter speaks to me, I listen. Maybe sometimes with only half an ear, when I'm in a middle of a project, but I listen." With a look of contempt he turned and took a few steps away. "Are you questioning my parenting ability?" He hated the hint of vulnerability that had crept into his voice. Even he, Mr. Advocate for Single Fatherhood, had doubts sometimes.

"Good Lord, no!" She stood up, hoping that she hadn't completely antagonized him. That was a mistake she couldn't afford, not when one of her students was at stake. "Please, Mr. Ferguson, you're misunderstanding."

"What precisely am I misunderstanding, Miss Walker?"

"The gravity of the situation. If Callie isn't having problems with articulation at home and is only demonstrating these disorders at school, I would say we have a major problem here."

Mitch cocked a brow. "Really?"

"Does your daughter know you were coming to see me today?"

"No. I saw no need to mention it to her until I knew what the problem was."

"Good." Hillary looked around the room. "Do you have an extra five minutes to spare?"

"For my daughter I have a lifetime to spare."

Hillary's smile was slow and sweet in coming. Mitch Ferguson was one hell of a father. "I know this is a bit unorthodox, but please bear with me." She walked over to a wall phone and dialed an extension. "Gladys, could you please contact Mrs. Bowater's room and have her send Callie Ferguson down to my room for a moment?" Her gaze held Mitch's questioning look. "Thank you."

She hung up the phone and smiled. "Callie will be here in a minute," she said, quickly opening the nearby closet door. "I want you to hide in here and listen."

"You want me to spy on my daughter?"

"No, I want you to listen. That's all." She handed him his coat and nodded toward the closet. "There's no way I can explain what's been happening this past week. I want you to hear it for yourself."

"I don't see how—"

"Please, for Callie's sake."

Mitch sighed. He would do anything for his daughter, including standing in a closet just to listen. "Fine, but the listening had better be pretty interesting, or I'm going to articulate some action of my own." Holding his jacket, he stepped behind the door.

Hillary frowned, praying for this to work. She turned to her seat and had just sat down when a tiny knock sounded on her door. "Come in, Callie."

"You wanted to thee me, Mith Walkel?"

Hillary smiled. There was no way Mitch Ferguson could not pick up on the problem now. "I have something for your father to sign. Could you take it home tonight for me?"

"Thure. Don't you want to thee im?"

"There's no need for a conference at this point, Callie. All I need is his signature on this form." She folded a piece of paper into thirds, stapled it shut, and wrote *Mr. Ferguson* on it.

Callie took the paper and chewed on her lower lip. "No converenth?"

Hillary raised a brow at the disappointment in the child's voice. Most kids grew nervous when an upcoming conference was mentioned, not when there *wasn't* going to be one. "Do you think I should call in your dad and discuss your lessons with him?"

Callie's gaze fell to the toe of her sneaker. "Well . . ."

This was getting stranger and stranger. First Callie began mispronouncing words at school, and now she was practically begging for her father to come in for a conference. "How about if I promise to think about it?"

Callie's smile was angelic, showing off the latest gap in her teeth. "He come in anytime to thee you."

"I'm sure he would." She watched as Callie headed for the door. "Thank you, Callie."

The little girl's smile was still radiant as she waved. "Ank you, Mith Walkel." The long brown ponytail was the last thing to disappear from sight.

Hillary sat there and waited for Mitch to step out of the closet. When he didn't, she said softly, "She's gone."

Mitch slowly reappeared, placed his jacket over the back of a chair, and made his way over to the wall of windows overlooking the parking lot. He jammed his hands into the pockets of jeans and stared at the assortment of cars. If he hadn't heard it himself, he would have never believed that that was his daughter talking a minute ago. He quickly thought back to the past week at home and dismissed the notion that he had overlooked the way she had been talking. He might have been extremely busy and preoccupied lately, and maybe he wasn't spending hours of *quality* time with his kids, but there was no way he could have missed this. Callie hadn't talked like that at home.

His first reaction was to shake Miss Articulation herself and demand to know what she and the school had done to his baby. A more reasonable response was to acknowledge the problem and figure out what was going on. Callie had sounded like a three-year-old practicing baby talk.

Hillary stared at his slumped shoulders. "I gather Callie hasn't been talking like that at home, has she?"

"No." He turned from the window. "How long has this been going on?"

"She started it on Monday. Mrs. Bowater and I have talked it over, and we can't find one thing different here at school that would cause such a change. Callie is well adjusted, has made many new friends, and has shown signs of above-average intelligence." Hillary glanced at the evaluation form she had filled out on Callie Wednesday morning. "We were hoping you would be able to shed some light on the matter."

"It has to be a problem at school. She doesn't talk like that at home."

Hillary avoided his gaze and doodled on the corner of the file. "She seems to be crying out for attention." She waited for the explosion. When none came, she glanced up and was amazed to see the beginning of a smile teasing the corner of his mouth.

"Are you sure it isn't just a phase she's going through?" he asked.

"A phase?"

"You sound like one of those child-rearing books that classifies everything a kid does into phases. I think parents should have their own phases. Like the never-getting-a-full-night's-sleep phase, acid-indigestion phase, the gray-hair phase, the famous I-can't-believe-I'm-a-parent-to-a-teenager phase, and then back to the never-getting-a-full-night's-sleep phase."

Hillary laughed. "How many child-rearing books have you read?"

"Dozens." Mitch sat back down across from her. He loved the way her spontaneous laughter had filled the room, and just for an instant it lightened his worry about Callie. "I've read everything from Dr. Spock to *Parents' Guide to Tough Love.*"

"Tough Love? Your son, Ethan, is only nine years old!"

"I'm preparing for the worst," he said with a smile.

Lord, with a smile like that the man could sell lacy undergarments to a nun. With a faint wave of her hand, to circulate some much-needed air, Hillary looked down to study the report. Only one thing should be on her mind, and it definitely shouldn't be lacy undergarments or Mitchell Ferguson. It should be her student Callie.

Needing to feel every bit the professional, she picked up a pair of glasses lying on top of a pile of papers and slipped them on. "After evaluating and listening closely to Callie I came to the conclusion that she's purposely trying to talk like that. She's slower in her speech, which indicates she's thinking about what she's going to say before she says it. On a couple of occasions Mrs. Bowater or I have heard her speak quite clearly when she thought no adult was around."

"Just like at home."

"Precisely."

Frustrated, Mitch ran a hand through his hair. "Why would she do it only part of the time?"

"I think she gave me a clue a couple of minutes ago." She had Mitch's full attention now. "How is Ethan as a student?"

"Average to above-average grades, prefers recess to math class, excels in gym, and hates music class. Why?"

"Does he have a problem with discipline?"

"Not yet, but I've noticed a distinctive devilish gleam in his eyes that tells me in a couple of years he'll be questioning every authority figure in sight."

"You haven't had to come in for a special conference on him or spend extra time with him studying?"

"No. Where is this heading, Miss Walker?"

"Callie doesn't have any other brothers or sisters?"

"None."

"What about stepsiblings?" Seeing the negative shake of his head, she quickly added, "Either in the past, present, or future?"

"No." He almost chuckled at the disappointment that flashed across her face. The huge owlish glasses she had put on made her eyes look larger, making every emotion there easier to read. "The clue didn't pan out?"

"No. Callie seemed awfully eager for you to come in for a conference. If Ethan required extra parental support and was receiving additional attention, it could explain why Callie wanted a conference."

Mitch frowned. "I haven't been any help to you, have I?" He glanced at Callie's folder. "Until you called, I hadn't even realized there was a problem." With a muttered oath he stood up. "Some father I am."

"Mr. Ferguson, don't beat yourself over the head with this. It's obviously a school problem, which means it's my problem."

"Any problem concerning my daughter is *my* problem."

Hillary admired the stubborn streak of responsibility running through him. Some parents would just walk away and say fine, you straighten it out. Others would want to call in every kind of specialist and demand the child be psychoanalyzed. Not Mitch, he wanted to be right on top of any problems. "How about if we compromise and we both work on figuring it out?"

Mitch stared at Hillary. He hadn't shared the responsibility of solving one of his kids' problems with anyone since his wife died five years ago. When one of his kids had a problem, they always came to him. He tried but failed to ignore the little voice in his head that asked, *So why didn't Callie come to you this time?* Maybe it was time he learned to accept someone else's help. "So where do we start?"

Hillary smiled. For a minute there she thought he was going to tell her to mind her own business. "I was hoping you could tell me."

Mitch sighed. Talk about the blind leading the blind. "What would happen if Callie had to face you and me together at the same time?"

"I don't know. She would have to go one way or the other, I guess." Hillary removed her glasses and absently chewed on the plastic earpiece. "Maybe I should have had you sitting here when she came down. Now it's too late. It'll have to wait until Monday."

"Maybe not. Will you be at the football game tonight? I promised the kids I'd take them to see the Cornfield Eagles play."

"I wasn't planning on it." The thought of meeting Mitch Ferguson outside of school was unsettling. Tempting as all get-out, but unsettling.

"Heavy date?" Why he was pushing the subject? Just because he didn't date didn't mean the rest of the world had stood still. Hillary obviously had other plans for Friday night.

"No."

"No date?" He couldn't believe that. Were the men this far south blind or just plain stupid?

"No, I had other plans." *Like washing my hair, pigging out on mint-chocolate-chip ice cream, and finishing the murder mystery I started last night.* Unresolved murders made her edgy all day.

She glanced down at Callie's folder. Mitch was right. Why wait until Monday? It wasn't as though he were asking her out on a date, he was only concerned about his daughter. "I guess it wouldn't hurt if I showed up at the game tonight. I haven't seen the high school team play once this year."

Mitch picked up his jacket as a wave of unexpected excitement quivered through him. "We'll meet you at the ticket booth at quarter to seven. Remember, you have to come up to us, because as far as Callie knows, we've never met."

"But . . ." She had only been planning to accidentally bump into him and Callie sometime during the game, not join his family for the evening.

He quickly headed out the door before she could change her mind. "Don't be late, or I won't buy you any hot dogs."

Hillary snapped her mouth closed and stared at

the empty doorway. She had been conned. Well, maybe conned was too strong a word, but Mitchell Ferguson was beginning to throw a little bit too much weight around for her taste. If it weren't for Callie's obvious cry for help, she'd leave Mr. Gorgeous Body standing outside the ticket booth all night long.

Mitch buttoned his coat against the wind, slid his hands into the pockets, and started the leisurely walk home. Half an hour ago he had jogged this same path hurrying to keep his appointment. Now he could take his time and enjoy the beauty of fall. The air was crisp, the leaves crunched under his feet, and life seemed a little brighter after his meeting Hillary. Callie's problem still perplexed him though. He knew his daughter had adjusted well to their recent move to Kansas county, Maryland, and had made many new friends. So why this cry for attention? And why was this cry directed toward her speech teacher?

With a kick he sent a pile of leaves flying into the air. Why had it become so important that Hillary Walker meet them at the game? Callie's problem could have waited till Monday. A frown pulled at his mouth as he sent another pile of leaves scattering on the wind. What was it about Hillary Walker that had finally penetrated his dormant libido? For the past five years he had worked side-by-side with a handful of beautiful, intelligent women, but none had stirred the desire that a prim-and-proper schoolteacher had.

Tonight not only was it going to be interesting to find out what Callie did, but he also couldn't wait to see the speech teacher outside the classroom.

Somehow the prim-and-proper-schoolmarm image just didn't suit the lady wearing black stockings with a faintly visible flower above the ankle. He wondered how many people never even noticed that intriguing flower.

Two

"Look, Dad, there's Miss Walker!" Ethan eagerly pulled his father's hand and tugged him toward Hillary.

Mitch had already seen the speech teacher making her way toward them. Even all bundled up against the evening cold, she looked irresistible. She had exchanged her proper suit for a knee-length teal-colored winter jacket, jeans, and sneakers. Her hair was pulled back into a thick braid that reached halfway down her back, and her cheeks were rosy from the wind. She looked kissable and good enough to eat. A very bad combination if he was expected to behave himself tonight. His howling hormones still hadn't calmed down from this afternoon. This evening wasn't officially a date, but it was the closest thing to one that he'd had since before his marriage.

He glanced down at Callie and was amazed to

see her usually smiling face scrunched up with distress. "What's wrong, honey?"

Callie shook her head and hid behind his legs as Hillary approached.

"Hi, Miss Walker, this is my dad," Ethan said, pulling on Mitch's hand.

Mitch switched his gaze from Callie's bent head to the woman standing in front of him. "Hello, I'm Mitch Ferguson. You must be Callie's speech teach."

Glancing at the barely visible Callie, Hillary extended her hand. "Yes, I am. Why don't you call me Hillary," she said, sending Mitch a silent question about his daughter's obvious reluctance to greet her. She frowned when Mitch merely shrugged in response. Taking the bull by the horn, she lowered her gaze to the child. "Hello, Callie. You didn't tell me you were a football fan."

Callie turned murderous eyes on Ethan, whose face held a positively angelic expression.

Mitch looked from his son to his daughter. He was beginning to smell a rat, or more accurate, two little rats. "Hillary, why don't you join us? I'm always interested in getting to know my kids' teachers."

Hillary was tempted to make up some excuse and refuse the invitation, but she was intrigued by Callie's silent treatment. Was this the same girl who hours before had wanted her father to come in for a conference? Whatever was going on was definitely strange. "If you're sure I won't be intruding?"

Ethan piped up before his father could answer. "Hey, that'll be neat, Miss Walker." He kicked his sister in the shins and returned her hateful stare. "Won't it, Callie?"

Hopping on one leg, Callie moved to the other side of her father. "Yeah."

Mitch bit the inside of his cheek to keep from laughing. There was discord among the troops. "Ethan, don't kick your sister. Hillary's going to think I didn't teach either of you manners." He glanced at the rapidly filling stadium and the dwindling line in front of the ticket booth. "We'd better get going before all the good seats are taken."

Hillary followed Mitch and Callie and glanced down at Ethan, who'd latched himself to her side. She had to agree with Mitch's earlier statement—the devil was definitely dancing in his eyes. She had noticed those same demons dancing in Mitch's eyes earlier this afternoon. Like father, like son.

Mitch purchased the tickets and led the way up to an empty row near the fifty-yard line. Hillary spread out the blanket she had brought along over the wooden bench seats, and with a stubborn tilt of her chin strategically placed Ethan and Callie between them. If there was one thing she'd learned in her thirty-one years, it was never to mix her personal feelings with her professional ones. She had agreed to meet Mitch at this game for one reason, Callie. The child was clearly crying out for help. She glanced at the little girl sitting next to Mitch. Callie hadn't spoken more than one word since they'd met in front of the ticket booth. Maybe this accidental meeting was a bad idea.

"Hey, Dad, can me and Callie have a dollar for some candy?"

Mitch pulled a bill out of his pocket and handed it to his son. "Just buy one and split it between you. I want you to save some room for hot dogs later."

As the children disappeared from sight, the high school's marching band came trooping onto the field playing an off-key version of "We're Off to See the Wizard." Hillary shook her head. Someone really should have a talk with the band director. Just because the town's name was Oz didn't mean that every year the band had to play the same songs from *The Wizard of Oz* over and over again. But it wasn't just the band that had the fixation; the entire town had it too. Last Halloween she had handed out three quarters of her trick-or-treat candy to scarecrows, lions, and tin men, and she personally knew five students who owned dogs named Toto. When she had moved here three years ago, after the scandal, Oz had seemed like a blessing with all its idiosyncrasies. No one would notice one very tarnished speech teacher, she hoped, and no one had. She had kept her personal life separate from her job at Oz Elementary School, and her persistence had paid off. Her world was now filled with peace and security, and if loneliness sometimes intruded, it was a small price to pay.

Hillary glanced at Mitch and frowned. The physical attraction she felt toward him could only be chalked up to the latest bout of loneliness that had entered her life on her thirty-first birthday last month. It had been a long time since she'd felt the heat of desire, and Mitch was quickly stirring the ashes back to life, something she couldn't afford. Once, she had impulsively given in to passion and had suffered as a result. She knew never to make that mistake again. With Mitch the best solution was to put as much distance between him and herself as the town of Oz would allow until she could regain her balance. And right now, that meant leaving the game as soon as possible.

Mitch turned to Hillary to make a comment on the band's rendition of "Follow the Yellow Brick Road," but the words died on his lips when he saw the look of panic in her eyes. "Hillary?"

"I've got to go. This was all a mistake."

He slid closer, eliminating the space between them. "I think I've figured it out, and it wasn't a mistake. I'm sure Callie will be talking normally by Monday morning."

Hillary blinked. "Callie?" Lord, how could she have forgotten the reason she was there? Mitch hadn't invited her to the football game because he was attracted to her. He was only concerned about his daughter. The warm feeling that seeped through her bones whenever he glanced at her was a figment of her imagination. His eyes didn't sparkle with hidden desires, and this breathlessness afflicting her body could be hypertension. Maybe she was developing some fatal heart disease at the age of thirty-one, one that affected her mind as well as her estrogen level.

Quickly recovering, Hillary said, "Callie hasn't spoken more than one word since I got here."

"I know. She's caught in her own trap. She can't talk normally or you would notice, and if she goes into her baby routine, I would notice."

"So why is she doing it?"

"I believe Ethan put her up to it."

"Ethan?"

"Yeah, Ethan." He saw his son and daughter making their way back up the bleachers and moved over to where he had been before. "I'll explain it all to you later."

He caught the crushed look on Ethan's face as the boy noticed the space between him and Hillary. After directing a curious glance at him, Ethan sat down next to Hillary and asked her who she thought was the greatest quarterback in NFL history. Callie silently contemplated the fluorescent orange laces on her sneakers.

The game started, and Mitch alternated his attention between the play on the field, his kids, and the intriguing woman two youngsters away. Why had there been a touch of panic in her eyes? Why had she declared the whole evening a mistake when she hadn't been thinking of Callie at all? But most important, he wondered what the prim-and-proper schoolmarm would do if he hauled her into his arms and ravaged her delectable mouth with hot, moist kisses until Christmas.

As the first quarter got off to a slow start, Mitch silently vowed he would have a couple of those questions answered by the end of the night.

Ethan climbed in the minivan after Callie and slammed the door shut. "See, I told you it would work."

Callie watched as her father walked Miss

Walker two rows back to her car. "He keeps looking at me funny."

"That's because you weren't talking."

Callie returned the kick she received earlier. "You know why."

Ethan let the kick slide for once and rubbed his shin. "He was only looking at you. He wasn't mad." Their plan was beginning to work. By Christmas Miss Walker was going to be their mom. He smiled into the darkness. Having a teacher for a mom could have some neat benefits—like no teacher would dare give him a bad grade for fear of having his new mom get mad at them. "She passed the number-four question."

"The one about baking good things to eat?" Callie asked eagerly.

"No, the one about knowing the starting quarterbacks in the NFL." Ethan turned around and spotted his father walking back toward the van. "She liked Montana the best though. I told her he was getting old, but she kept saying something about experience."

Callie glared at her brother and kicked the seat in front of her. She didn't care about any stupid quarterbacks or football. She wanted to know if Miss Walker could bake fancy cupcakes just like the kind Dorothy's mother had made for their class to celebrate Dorothy's birthday. The girl had bragged that only her mother could bake them. Callie's birthday was coming up right after Christmas, and she wanted a mother who could outbake smartypants Dorothy's. Having her dad pick up cupcakes from a bakery just wasn't the same as having a real mom bake them for you.

* * *

Mitch parked the van and studied the house in front of him. It was neat and small, just the kind he pictured Hillary living in. After he had gotten the kids to bed, he had looked up Hillary's address in the telephone book, and informed Eunice that he was going out for a while.

Now, as he got out of the van and made his way up the brick walk to the front door, he was thankful lights were still glowing from a couple of downstairs windows.

Barging in on someone unannounced at ten-thirty at night went against good manners, but he had to talk to Hillary. He had gotten the feeling Hillary was running scared. Running from what he didn't know, but the who had definitely been him. She couldn't have gotten away fast enough tonight after the game.

He pressed the doorbell, and after several moments, the porch light flared on. "Who is it?"

"Mitch Ferguson," he answered.

Hillary opened the door as far as the security chain would allow. The precaution was a leftover habit from having lived in Baltimore all those years. When she'd walked into the hardware store in Oz and asked for one, Don, the owner, had been appalled. But Hillary insisted on buying one and installed it herself. Now she peered out onto the lit porch and sighed. Sure enough, Mitch stood there, looking incredibly sexy. Tonight she would have rather seen a gang of burglars and their moving van backing into her driveway than Mitch standing at her door. Burglars she could fight, Mitch she wasn't too sure about. "Yes?"

"Can we talk?"

She unfastened the chain. He was right, they really should discuss Callie. "Would you like to come in? I was just having a cup of coffee, would you care for one?"

"That sounds great," Mitch said as he stepped into the living room. He unzipped his jacket and laid it across the back of the blue plaid couch as she disappeared into the kitchen. Hillary's living room was crowded with country furnishings. A hand-stitched Amish quilt took up an entire wall while two blue print chairs clustered around the couch and pine end tables. A stuffed goose stood watch over the hallway, and what appeared to be a pig lay contentedly under one of the tables chewing on a wooden apple. Baskets were filled with magazines, balls of yarn, and one held a ceramic chicken surrounded by plastic eggs. Hillary's living room contained more animals than Old MacDonald's farm. Even her lamp shades had sheep on them.

"Here we are." Hillary set a tray with coffee down on a table. "I hope you don't mind instant."

"Instant is fine." Mitch sat down on the couch and hid his smile as she took one of the chairs. "I see you like animals."

Hillary glanced around the room with pride. Years of searching through flea markets, visiting antique and craft shops, and going to craft shows had paid off. Her home was exactly as she envisioned it should be. Maybe it was becoming a bit overcrowded, but she couldn't seem to pass up on any cute critter that caught her eye. "I was born and raised in Baltimore. The city isn't any place to raise animals."

"Not even a cat?"

"My mom's allergic to cats." Hillary frowned. She hadn't meant to say anything remotely personal. It was all Mitch's fault. She knew he was going to be trouble the minute he walked into her classroom this afternoon. After spending one evening with him and his children, she was ready to spill her entire life story. Wouldn't that shock the very devil that sometimes danced in Mitch's eyes!

She quickly picked up her cup of coffee and took a sip of the steaming liquid. She needed to get Mitch out of her house and life before he jeopardized her newly found peace. "You said something about knowing why Callie was talking like a two-year-old?"

Mitch followed her lead and picked up his cup. "I've been trying to think of a nicer way of saying this than just blurting out the truth, but I can't."

Hillary's curious gaze collided with his. "I always prefer the truth."

Mitch sighed and replaced the cup on the tray. He clasped his hands together and sat up straighter. "It seems that Ethan and Callie overheard our housekeeper and my sister, Ronnie, talking the other week." He cleared his throat. "Their topic of conversation was my poor disposition in life recently."

Hillary cocked one finely arched brow.

"You see, I've been under a lot of strain lately. We just moved here from Chicago in August, and

Eunice, that's our housekeeper, has taken it upon herself to repaint every room in the house for me. So far the living room has been painted three different colors, none of which has suited her yet. Ronnie moved out of her apartment in Baltimore and came to live with us because she feels the kids need a stable female role model in their life. Only problem is, Ronnie works nights and sleeps all day. The kids rarely see her, and I worry constantly about her safety. I left a very good job I held for ten years to fulfill a dream. It's not easy starting from scratch when you have two kids, a housekeeper, and a mortgage depending on you."

"I don't suppose it is." Hillary's heart gave a tiny tug in the direction it had no business going. "I can see why you have been under a great deal of strain lately, but I still don't get the connection with Callie's speech."

"This is the embarrassing part. It seems Eunice and Ronnie's solution to my problem is a girlfriend." It wasn't their exact wording, but he could tell from Hillary's expression she got the general drift. He knew for a fact his kids hadn't overheard that particular conversation, because he had just seen them off to school and had come back into the house before heading for his lab in the garage as he usually did. Ethan and Callie weren't looking for a girlfriend for him, they were searching for a mother. Both had been asking, subtly and sometimes not so subtly, for a mother for over a year now. He had tried to explain to them that they both had had a mother who had loved them very much, and he felt no desire to try to replace her.

Amazed, Hillary sat there in silence for a full minute before saying, "You mean to tell me Callie was trying to play matchmaker?"

"Afraid so. I can't blame it all on Callie, though. Ethan was the mastermind behind the plan."

"Why me?"

The devil was back in his eye. "Because Ethan has extremely good taste."

Hillary shot him a warning glance as she put down her coffee.

"I guess being new in town, they started with who they knew. How many single teachers are there?"

"Three, counting myself. Miss Puffin who's sixty-five if she's a day, and Miss Battson."

"What's wrong with her?"

"Nothing's wrong with Miss Battson. She's a very fine teacher and a nice lady who just happens to see the world through different eyes than the rest of us."

"What kind of world does she visualize?"

"One that's governed by music. Miss Battson doesn't talk to you, she sings to you."

"All the time?"

"Miss Battson believes life is one big musical, and she has the starring role."

Mitch chuckled. "I now see why Ethan and Callie picked you."

Hillary tried to control the heated flush sweeping up her cheeks and failed. To be set up by a seven- and a nine-year-old was unnerving. She pulled together every ounce of sophistication she owned and gracefully tried to make light of the situation. "I'm flattered that Ethan and Callie chose me, but as you can see, it just wouldn't work."

"Why not?"

Hillary's mouth opened in astonishment, and when she spoke, her voice rose in outrage. "You can't be serious."

Mitch leaned back against the sofa in a deceptively casual pose. His heart was pounding, and his palms were starting to sweat. During the drive over he had come to the conclusion that his interest in Hillary wasn't because she was Callie's teacher. He was determined to get to know Hillary the woman. The woman who finally awoke the flesh-and-blood man inside him. What made her so different from every other woman he'd had contact with in the last five years? "I happen to think the kids' plan has a lot of merit."

"Well, think again." Hillary jumped to her feet and started to pace the small, crowded room.

"Did I mention that at times Ethan shows signs of being a genius?" He ignored her glare. "It seems my son and I have the same taste in women."

"Ethan still thinks girls have cooties."

Mitch laughed. "I'm sure it's just a phase he's going through." He nervously tidied the tray and carried it into the kitchen.

Wooden, metal, ceramic, and hand-knitted cows covered every available space. The teakettle was of a black-and-white holstein pattern, and even the cookie jar had udders. The entire room looked like a cow convention had been booked there and forgot to leave. "You obviously aren't married." Hillary shot him another irritated look. "No offense, Hillary, but I don't know too many men who would appreciate eating in a dairy barn every day." *Definitely not your smoothest line, Mitch old boy.*

"I'll worry about that if I get married." She didn't like the fact that he easily jumped to the conclusion that she wasn't married. She wasn't bad-looking, was blessed with her fair share of intelligence, and held a respectable job. If she wanted to find a husband, it shouldn't be that difficult. She just wasn't interested in tying any matrimony knots.

Mitch noted the "*if* I get married." She hadn't said "when I get married." Interesting. Most people automatically assumed they would marry someday, but not Hillary. "I haven't noticed any signs of a boyfriend."

"Could be because there isn't one." Hillary folded her arms across her chest and watched as Mitch reached for his coat. His sweater pulled up with the movement, revealing faded jeans that molded to his tight rear. She closed her eyes against the appealing sight but couldn't help giving a silent prayer of thanks to the cotton growers of America. Only jeans could have shown off that display of masculine buns to their perfection.

"Then there's no reason why you can't have dinner with me tomorrow night." Mitch slipped on the jacket as his nerves started to fray. This dating business could be hell on a man's ego.

Hillary snapped back to reality with a thud. Mitch had just asked her out. "You would date a woman because your kids picked her out?" She knew she wasn't going to go out with Mitch, but she felt insulted anyway.

"Hell, no. I would do almost anything for my kids, but dating isn't one of them." He closed the distance between them. "Having dinner with you tomorrow night is strictly my own idea." He gently reached up and tucked a wayward auburn curl behind her ear. It felt soft and airy against his finger.

She steadied herself against the tender gesture. She couldn't afford to weaken now.

Mitch's finger lightly traced the curve of her lower lip. "Will you have dinner with me?"

Hillary sank her teeth onto the trail of warmth his finger left behind. The situation was becoming increasingly dangerous. Her body and heart were screaming *yes*, while her head was telling her *no*. God didn't grant fools second chances. Her common sense won the battle. "I'm sorry, but no."

A faint smile played across his mouth. The first woman in five years to ignite any kind of feelings inside him was turning him down. "Why not?" He gently tilted up her chin and forced her to meet his gaze.

Panic started setting in. Why couldn't he accept a *no* and be on his way? "Maybe I don't want to go out with you."

When Mitch saw the fear in her eyes, he knew he hadn't been mistaken earlier at the football game. Hillary was scared of something, so much so that she was denying the physical attraction between them. "I think you want to, but you're afraid."

"Afraid?"

"Yes. And I think it's of me."

"Of you? Don't be ridiculous."

"Prove it by having dinner with me tomorrow night." Mitch followed every emotion flickering across her face and held his breath. He understood about running scared; he had been hiding from life since his wife died. But something about Hillary made coming out of his self-imposed exile worthwhile. His body had given him that message this afternoon; now his head was echoing the point.

Hillary knew she had lost the battle when he challenged her. She couldn't resist a dare. What could one little dinner hurt? She'd go out with him and have a mediocre time. If he asked her out again, she would refuse, and he wouldn't be able to insinuate she was frightened of him or any other man. Hillary shifted her gaze from beyond his shoulder to his gentle eyes. The devils weren't anywhere in sight. "Dinner sounds lovely."

Mitch released the breath he had been holding. He didn't know why she'd changed her mind, but he wasn't going to push his luck. Impulsively he pressed a soft kiss against her mouth. "Seven?"

"Seven," Hillary whispered.

Mitch opened the front door, knowing he had to beat a hasty exit. The kiss he'd given her had been no more than brotherly, but it had been enough to stir him to the point where his arousal strained against the front of his jeans. *If she wasn't running scared before, she surely would be at the sight of his desire.* His voice was thick as he muttered, "Sleep tight," and closed the door behind him.

Hillary stared at the door and touched her lips with the tip of her finger. His gentle kiss was still there. She could feel it. The tender contact had surprised her in more ways than one. It had been totally unexpected, and it wasn't the type of kiss she would have anticipated from a man like Mitch. During the football game, which the Eagles won after making a resounding comeback, Mitch had not only plied her with hot dogs, coffee, and a chewy brownie smothered in walnuts, but he had also filled her mind with wickedly sinful thoughts that all started with his kisses and ended somewhere between satin sheets.

The kiss Mitch had left her with was as far removed from satin sheets as one could get. So why was her body responding as if to a four-alarm fire?

With a frown she locked the door, reinserted the chain, and turned off the lights. Sleeping tight was going to be an impossibility. Just plain sleeping was going to be a minor miracle. She never should have accepted Mitch's challenge. She had a feeling she was going to lose more than her hard-won peace to Mitch's charm.

Three

Mitch glanced around the Ruby Slipper with interest. He had questioned three different people in town as to where the best place to have dinner was, and all had answered The Ruby Slipper if he wanted elegant food and plenty of privacy. If he was interested in a *nice* time, they all highly recommended the Horse of a Different Color. With visions in his mind of waiters dressed up as scarecrows and the house specialty named the Wicked Witch of the West burger, he chose elegance and privacy over "nice." He might be a little rusty on the dating scene, but he wasn't stupid.

The Ruby Slipper, located just out of town, closer to Washington, D.C., sat on top of a hill overlooking the entire town of Oz and the surrounding rolling hills. It was an early 1800s Federal-style mansion that spoke of the graceful elegance of a bygone era. Mitch couldn't have imagined a more perfect setting for Hillary and their first date.

He glanced at the woman sitting across from him reading the menu and felt a sense of pride. She was his date. More than a few male heads had turned as they had made their way across the floor to the table. Hillary was, by far, the most beautiful woman in the restaurant, and she didn't seem to notice. The black dress she was wearing was simple and discreet in its design. He never had been one for keeping up with fashion, but what Hillary did for that simple black dress could make a grown man cry. If his sleeping hormones hadn't already awakened, the alarm surely would have sounded at the sight of Hillary's outfit to-night. Shimmery black material clung to her every curve like an Indy race car. Tiny diamond earrings glistened in the candlelight, and the deep red shade of her lipstick drew his gaze to her full lips like a magnet. Hunger coiled through his body. He wanted to savor those ruby-red lips like a fine wine. He was becoming intoxicated just looking at her.

Hillary slowly lowered the menu and glanced around the room. The Ruby Slipper was as elegant as she had heard. Mitch's challenge was going to cost him a bundle. She hadn't exactly expected to be taken to a fast-food restaurant, but one of the most exclusive restaurants within a hundred miles was surprising. Didn't he know about the Horse of a Different Color? How was she supposed to have a mediocre time at the Ruby Slipper? Only a sea slug would consider anything about the Ruby Slipper mediocre.

She had already noticed that Mitch fit in per-fectly with the surroundings. His gray suit hadn't come off any rack, and his shoes screamed hand-made from Italy. Yet he drove an economy-minded minivan. Intrigued in spite of herself, she leaned in closer and whispered, "Can I ask you a question?"

Mitch smiled at her hushed tone. There wasn't a person near enough to overhear them even if they were talking in normal voices. "Ask away."

"What exactly do you work on?" As far as she knew, he could be on anything from fertilizer to a cure for cancer. Chemistry was such a broad field.

"Garbage."

Hillary was mentally thrown off balance. Mitch didn't seem like a man who was unhappy in his work. "I didn't ask what you thought about it, I asked what you're currently working on."

Mitch chuckled. He loved getting people's reaction to that answer. "That's what I work on, garbage."

She raised one brow. "People must be throwing away some *interesting* things nowadays."

He threw back his head and laughed. "I have a doctor's degree in polymer chemistry. I'm currently working on the breakdown of plastics for recycling purposes."

"You're an environmentalist?"

"I was there for the first Earth Day. I thought it was a good idea then, but I think it's a better idea now. I mistakenly took a couple of wrong turns down the career path, but I'm on the right path now."

"Callie told me you work at home."

"I do. I have a lab set up in the garage for most

of my work. When I need more sophisticated equipment, I can always run into D.C."

A waiter approached their table, and after they gave their order, she asked, "Whom do you work for? The government?"

"Afraid not. I work for an environmental group called Greenleaves. It's a small but growing group of concerned citizens who are tired of waiting for the government to solve our planet's problems."

Hillary gave a low whistle. "I've heard of it. From what I've read, Greenleaves is pulling together only the top people in their fields to accomplish its goals."

Mitch raised his glass of wine. "Thank you. I believe you just gave me a compliment."

A loud, boisterous laugh accompanied by a high-pitched giggle filled the room. Hillary's eyes narrowed as she noticed an elderly congressman playing footsie with a Marilyn Monroe look-alike at the next table. The look-alike was definitely not the congressman's wife, and this particular congressman appeared on the front page of more tabloids than Elizabeth Taylor or Oprah Winfrey.

She ignored the loud couple and nervously pleated the napkin in her lap. She didn't want Mitch to be so saintly. Why couldn't he be working on bug repellent or a new, improved laundry detergent? It was going to be hard enough resisting his good looks and charm, but throw a heap of moral convictions on top of that, and she was in deep trouble. Mitch was turning into a walking fantasy. So what was he doing having dinner with her? Exciting, beautiful, and perfect women had to be knocking down his door for this chance.

The waiter returned with their food, and as Hillary dug into her meal, Mitch decided it was time to get to know a few things about her. So far all they had talked about was him. "So tell me, Hillary, why did you become a speech teacher?"

Hillary swallowed her first mouthful of trout and smiled. "I stutter."

Mitch's fork paused in midair as he stared at the beautiful woman across from him. "I beg your pardon?"

"I said I stutter." Noticing his look of total disbelief, she explained, "When I was five, I couldn't string more than three words together without stammering. The more frustrated I became, the worse the stuttering got."

Light dawned in Mitch's eyes. "You idealized the speech teacher who cured you and vowed to become one when you grew up."

Hillary burst out laughing, causing a few patrons to glance their way. "Lord, no!" She held her napkin to her lips trying to silence the remaining chuckles. "Sister Mary Theresa was an ogre. Every time I stammered, she whacked my knuckles with a wooden ruler."

"She hit you?" Mitch was appalled.

"It was either learn to talk properly or go through life with the knuckles of a baboon." She watched Mitch lower his fork to his plate. "Mitch, I'm teasing you. As soon as my parents found out what was happening, they took me out of Holy Redeemer and enrolled me in a public school, where I idealized my speech teacher and vowed to become one when I grew up."

Mitch waved his fork under her nose. "That was a terrible thing to do."

Hillary snatched the piece of meat off the tip of his fork with her teeth. "I couldn't resist. You seemed so sure of yourself."

"Did you really stutter?"

"Yes." She took a sip of wine. "I still do when I get excited."

Mitch stared at her lips and felt the quivering of desire shake his soul. "Define 'excited.'"

Hillary noticed the devils weren't dancing in his eyes any longer; they were smoldering. A fiery red swept up her cheeks as she remembered the last time she did stutter. It had been three years ago when she was still naive, and the whole world seemed perfect. Oh yes, she definitely did stutter, and Bruce had hated it. She lowered her gaze to her wineglass.

Accurately reading every emotion that passed across her face, Mitch felt jealousy tear at his gut. He wanted to be the man who had made her stutter. But at her obvious embarrassment, he reined in the emotion and changed the subject. He wanted Hillary to enjoy herself tonight, not regret that she agreed to this date. "I did notice that when the Eagles scored the first winning touchdown, you seemed at a loss for words."

"It was the shock," she said, thankful for something else to talk about.

"Shock?"

"I didn't want to mention it then, but in all the excitement of the game Ethan spilled half his soda down my leg."

It was Mitch's turn to be embarrassed. "Why didn't you tell me?"

"It was only soda." She speared another forkful of trout and glanced at his untouched plate. "You really ought to try your steak, it's delicious."

Mitch hid his smile of approval. Not many woman would brush off having cold soda dumped down their pant leg in November. Even his sister, who loved the kids, had been known to lose patience with them once in a while. Hillary's already golden halo just got a little brighter.

The meal passed quickly with Hillary answering more questions about herself and, in the process, revealing more about herself than she'd confided to anybody in Oz. It seemed so natural and easy to talk to Mitch. He possessed the lost art of listening—really listening to what a person said. He asked her about her family, her career, and even about the crazy assortment of animals decorating her home.

As the meal was cleared away, Hillary couldn't remember ever having enjoyed herself more on a date. Especially a first date—they always tended to be awkward and stiff. With Mitch she felt she could be herself. Maybe she had been hiding in the past long enough.

Mitch chuckled at the look of pure admiration gleaming in her eyes as the dessert tray was brought to their table. "Someone has a sweet tooth."

"This looks more exciting than watching the congressman nearly fall out of his chair," Hillary whispered, then selected a slice of raspberry-mousse pie.

Mitch indicated he wanted a small plate of assorted fruit. This date with Hillary had gone better than he had expected. When he had picked her up at seven sharp, he had caught the undercurrent of coolness in her greeting. He couldn't blame her. He had practically dared her to go out with him. Not the most romantic way to start the evening, but without the dare, he was sure there wouldn't have been an evening. Obviously she had been prepared to be polite and standoffish.

He hadn't really known what to expect from her. Not only was she gorgeous and sexy, but she had a sharp mind and one wicked sense of humor. No one could have sat within ten feet of her and not been drawn to her glow like a moth to a flame. The more she revealed, the more he wanted to know. He had never met such a fascinating woman, and he was nowhere near done exploring her uniqueness.

Hillary finished her dessert with a sigh. The night was coming to an end, and amazingly she wasn't ready for it. The food had been excellent, the scenery interesting, but it was the company that had been fascinating. She had been prepared to rebuff Mitch's every overture, but he hadn't made any. He had been the perfect gentleman.

She knew for a fact that he was a widower with two small children. His housekeeper was named Eunice, and was at least a dozen years older than he was; she either loved to paint or suffered bouts of color blindness. His sister, Ronnie, lived with them and had some career he strongly disapproved of. There was no hidden wife half the country away. There was nothing in his background that would cause a scandal if she continued to see him. The incident that ruined her life three years ago would never be repeated with Mitch. It had taken her years to scrape the mud off her name and pull her life back together. The lightest breath of scandal would never touch her again. She was safe in Oz.

Hillary gazed at the handsome man sitting across from her and felt immense pleasure. Not only was Mitch sexy and made her laugh, he was also caring. The tie he wore was more evidence of that trait. While the roomful of elegantly dress men favored ties in muted reds and conservative stripes, Mitch's was a wild print of endangered species. She owned a vest that virtually matched the print. For the first time in years she felt she could trust a man.

She finished her coffee and gazed warmly at him. "I had a wonderful time tonight."

He responded to the warmth like kindling to a match. His libido went up in flames. "I'm glad."

He was about to ask if she was willing to try it again, when all hell broke out in the kitchen. Raised voices and frantic shouting could be heard coming from the back of the mansion. Before anyone could move, a young man came bursting through the swinging doors wildly snapping pictures of anyone and everyone. Shouts of indignation filled the room along with howls of outrage. High-pitched feminine screams of surprise and nervous giggles battled against the already-rising volume. Within an instant the elegant Ruby Slipper had turned into chaos.

Chairs were upended, demands uttered while

flashes from the man's camera arced through the dimly lit room. Waiters and the kitchen staff converged on the room with the intent of capturing and disposing of the photographer.

Mitch swore as a number of patrons headed for the door. It was definitely time to beat a hasty retreat. He placed his napkin on the table and stood up. With a formal bow and a wicked smile, he indicated the exit. "Shall we, my dear?"

Hillary chuckled and lightly patted her lips with the linen napkin. With an air of total nonchalance at the surrounding mayhem, she rose. "Most definitely, kind sir."

Mitch had just pushed in his chair and was rounding the table to escort Hillary to the cloakroom when disaster struck. The maître d', engrossed in trying to grab the photographer, dashed across the room and crashed into Hillary. One of her legs shot up, and her arms flew wide as she fell backward, directly into the congressman's lap. Mitch made a wild grab for her, but only ended up grasping a delicate ankle in midair. He quickly released the ankle when he noticed the precarious position of her dress, and helped her to her feet.

Hillary felt the tide of embarrassment and outrage sweep to her face as she glared at the congressman. She wasn't positive, but she was pretty sure the lecherous fool had patted her bottom.

"Hillary, are you all right?" Mitch asked after he'd retrieved her handbag and handed it to her.

"I will be just as soon as I get out of here." She tugged on her dress. With a sweet smile she stepped closer to the congressman. "Thank you, kind sir, for the gallant use of your lap."

The congressman maintained his politically correct smile as her three-inch heel dug into his shoe. "It was my pleasure."

Hillary's eyes narrowed for a fraction of a second. "I'm sure it was." She turned and took Mitch's arm. "I'm ready whenever you are."

They walked out of the dining room as the nimble photographer hurled a table, avoided a dozen outstretched hands, and made a speedy exit out of the restaurant.

"Are you going to tell me what that was all about with the congressman?" Mitch asked twenty minutes later as he walked Hillary up the brick path to her front door. He had been too busy admiring the seductive view of her leg to see anything. But he sensed something happened.

"No, the problem is solved." She unlocked the door. "Want to come in for a quick cup of coffee?"

Mitch pushed away from the doorjamb and followed. Things had definitely improved since he'd picked her up at seven. "Sounds great," he answered, taking off his overcoat and laying it across the back of a chair. "Do you need any help?"

"No, make yourself at home." She hung up her coat and headed for the kitchen. "Unless you'd rather have your coffee in the dairy barn."

Mitch chose the black-and-white spotted room. Having coffee with her in there sounded homey and intimate. He sat on a stool at the counter and watched as she filled the kettle with water. Surrounded by cows, she should have looked out of place wearing a black cocktail dress and diamond earrings, but instead she looked sexy, warm, and comfortable. "So tell me, Hillary, why aren't you married?"

Spotted ceramic mugs shook in her hands before she placed them on the counter. She studied the black-and-white-tiled countertop and tried to regain her composure. Mitch had asked a very reasonable question, so why was she allowing the past to interfere? Hadn't she come to the conclusion tonight to give him and life a chance?

Mitch frowned at her silence. "Or have you been?"

"No," she said, giving a halfhearted laugh, "I've never been married." She measured instant coffee into the cups. "But I almost got married once."

"You were engaged?"

"Not exactly." *We were living together for a month while his wife was two thousand miles away caring for his eighteen-month-old son and carrying their second child.* She didn't want to talk about it any longer. She didn't want Mitch to know what kind of fool she had been. "Are you sure you don't mind instant?" she asked, getting the sugar bowl and taking a container of milk from the refrigerator.

"Positive." Mitch allowed the subject to be changed. "So whose picture do you think the photographer was after?"

Hillary shrugged her shoulders. The man had been running around the room snapping pictures of everyone, so it was hard to tell. But whoever it was, a scandal was sure to follow. "I hope they caught the photographer and destroyed all the film."

Mitch glanced curiously at her. "Why?"

"No one deserves to be hounded like that. Everyone's entitled to his or her privacy." She was an expert on scandals. She had lived through one.

He heard the pain and anguish in her voice and frowned. Something, or someone, had hurt her in the past. "I hadn't thought of it that way."

"No one ever does. Everyone loves a juicy story, be it truth or fiction." She handed him a cup filled with coffee. "It's only the innocent or the incredibly naive who get hurt by it all."

"Like you?"

Hillary stared at Mitch for a long time. If she was planning to allow this one date to turn into something more, she would have to tell him about Bruce sooner or later. She preferred later. It would take a lot of guts to admit to a man she was becoming extremely fond of that she'd been played for a fool. "Yeah, like me."

Mitch waited for her to continue, but she didn't. She obviously wanted to drop the subject. "I could never imagine you being naive, so I would have to say you were innocent." He took a sip of coffee and smiled. "So how do you think the Redskins will do this year?"

The next half hour was spent arguing football. Hillary was convinced that the Redskins would go all the way, while Mitch was a devoted Chicago Bears follower. They ended up agreeing that football was the greatest game ever played.

Afterward Mitch slowly made his way into the living room and pulled on his coat. He didn't want to overstay his welcome. Hillary was as skittish as a newborn colt, and gut instinct told him that rushing her would be the wrong move. He reached for her hand, slowly pulling her toward him, and smiled when she didn't back away. "I had a wonderful time tonight."

"So did I." She did something she had been dying to do all night: She lightly ran a finger down his jaw. The beginning of a rough stubble teased her. "It must have been the company."

He reached for the wandering fingertip and pressed a kiss on it. "Remind me to take you to the Ruby Slipper more often."

Hillary smiled as his lips caressed the palm of her hand.

"Did I tell you how beautiful you looked to-night?"

She felt a faint nip at her wrist, and her body immediately swayed forward to brush up against his. "Twice."

Mitch's body started to throb. He wanted her. He wanted her badly. "I'm trying to go real slow here, Hillary." His arms encircled her as he gazed at her upturned face. "I don't want to scare you."

She smiled seductively. "You won't."

His mouth swept down and one word was whispered against her waiting lips, "Good."

Hillary matched the desire of his kiss with a seductive sweep of her tongue over his lower lip. This was the kiss she had expected last night. This was how a man was supposed to kiss a woman. As if he meant it. She reached up and dug her fingers through his hair as the kiss deepened.

Everything that proclaimed her a woman rose up to meet the heated demand of his mouth.

His hands cupped her hips and brought her in contact with his arousal. When she rubbed up against him, his control nearly snapped. He broke the kiss and forced a couple of desperately needed inches between them. He would have liked nothing better than to carry her down the hallway to her bed. But Hillary wasn't a one-night stand or even a let's-go-to-bed-on-the-first-date type of woman. She was special. Besides, someone had hurt her once, and she was still leery. No matter how she responded in his arms, he had to go slow or he would lose her before he had a chance to understand her. "I think I should leave before this goes any further."

Hillary felt her already flushed face heat up more. He was right. This was getting totally out of hand. What was the matter with her? In another moment she would have been begging him to make love to her. She couldn't meet his gaze. "I think that would be for the best."

Mitch tilted up her chin and memorized every detail of her face. He liked the way her lips had become swollen from his kisses. She would go to sleep tonight with his mark on her. In a tender moment he bent and lightly stroked those swollen red lips with his tongue. "I'll call you tomorrow, okay?"

Her tongue followed the same path his had just taken. The embarrassment started to fade. "Okay."

Mitch opened the door and stepped out into the darkness while he still had control over his body.

A few more kisses like that one, and they wouldn't have made it past the goose. He would have laid down with her in the middle of the living room and given the funny farm something to gawk at.

Mitch stared at the newspaper clutched in his hand and cursed. The neighborhood in which Hillary's house was located was barely showing signs of life, and he doubted that Hillary herself was out of bed yet. He didn't want to be the one to show her the morning paper. In fact, given a choice, he would have rather been swimming in shark-infested waters or tobogganing down Mount Everest in a cardboard box than standing on Hillary's front porch at seven o'clock on this Sunday morning. The one thing he was positive would make her back away from him had happened. And it had happened in spades.

He rang the doorbell and waited. A couple of minutes later he rang it again. Hillary's sleepy voice came through the door: "Who is it?"

"Mitch." He hid the paper behind his back as she opened the door and stared sleepily up at him.

"What are you . . . ?"

"May I come in?"

"Sure," she said, pulling the sash on her white chenille robe tighter, then running her fingers through her tousled hair.

Mitch stepped inside and smiled at the picture she made standing there barefoot. "I take it you haven't seen the morning paper."

Hillary blinked and wondered if she were

dreaming. She said the first thing that came into her mind. "I need coffee."

He slapped the crumpled paper against his thigh before handing it to her. When delivering bad news, he found it was always better to get it over with fast. He hoped Hillary felt the same way. "You'd better look at this first. You might need something stronger to drink."

She glanced from his serious expression to the much-battered newspaper. She'd never had a premonition of disaster before today, but one hit her now. With shaking fingers she unfolded the paper and glanced at the front page. A picture of her sitting on the congressman's lap with her skirt hiked to midthigh and Mitch's hand grasping her ankle stared back at her. She read the bold black print above the photo before her fingers lost all feeling and the paper dropped to the floor: SCANDAL ROCKS OZ.

Four

Mitch grabbed her shoulders as every ounce of blood drained from her face. Staring at him with dazed green eyes, she spoke in a voice that sounded weak and pitiful. "This is even worse than the first time."

He walked her over to the sofa and sat her down. He didn't like the look of her complexion. She seemed ready to pass out. Mitch never had a woman faint on him before, and he wasn't relishing the idea right now. "Take a deep breath."

She didn't want to take a breath, deep or otherwise. She wanted to murder someone. She wanted to crawl back into bed and pull the covers up over her head and never see daylight again. How could life be so cruel? What had she ever done to deserve this?

Mitch relaxed as color flooded back into Hillary's cheeks. "How about I go make us some coffee?" She nodded, and he hurried from the room.

A few minutes later he returned, carrying a black-and-white tray. He frowned as he set it down. Hillary was reading the article underneath the picture. Most of it was about the congressman at the Ruby Slipper last night and how he flaunted his affairs for all of America to see, then went on to identify the woman sitting on the congressman's lap as a Ms. Bambi Galore, an exotic dancer at the famed Paradise Club.

Hillary meticulously folded the paper so the photo showed and placed it on the table. They hadn't even gotten her name right. Not sure if that was a blessing or not, she picked up her coffee and drank.

Mitch nervously sat down in a chair. Shouldn't Hillary be ranting and raving demanding a correction? He fidgeted with straightening the tray, newspaper, and the wooden ducks that were sitting on the table. Her silence was nerve-racking. "You can sue for libel."

She slowly shook her head. "It's not worth it." The idea had crossed her mind, but she had dismissed it as foolishness. She could prove she wasn't Ms. Bambi Galore with no problem, but the exposure would likely send reporters digging into her past and unearthing the scandal three years ago. It had been bad enough that practically the entire Baltimore School District and a quarter of the city knew the story, just by word of mouth. To have it plastered across every major newspaper in America would go beyond humiliation. Any story that involved a congressman and an exotic dancer would surely capture the nation's attention.

"What do you mean, it's not worth it?" Her picture had been smeared across the entire state and God knows where else, and all she could say was it's not worth it!

She swirled the coffee around in her cup and stared at the vortex. Life was sucking her back under again. She jumped as the shrill ringing of the phone split the silence. She didn't want to answer it. What if it was her parents? What if it was the head of the school board demanding to know what one of its teachers was doing on a congressman's lap? How in the hell was she going to explain it was all just an accident?

Mitch cursed as a troubled look came over Hillary. He needed to know what had happened in the past that still haunted her today, but first he had to stop the blasted phone from ringing. With an angry stride he marched into the kitchen, picked up the receiver, and barked, "Hello?"

Hillary wasn't sure if she was thankful or mad at Mitch for answering her phone. Half-curious, half-incensed, she listened to his one-sided conversation. He sounded indignant when he had to identify himself to the caller. A sad smile touched her mouth as he stated he was a friend. Last night they could have became lovers, but he was the one who had held back. This morning even the friendship would be gone. It was time to tell him about Bruce and the past. She had to make him understand why stirring up more trouble was out of the question.

She shook her head in disbelief as Mitch promised the caller that the problem would be rectified by tomorrow and hung up. "Who was that?" she asked when he marched back into the living room and sat down.

"Your brother."

Hillary groaned. It was going to be as bad as she first thought. She was surprised her parents hadn't called yet. Dad had a habit of sleeping in on Sunday morning, and her mother had probably fainted dead away on the kitchen floor by now. Why hadn't she been hatched from some incubator instead of real flesh-and-blood people? She didn't want to hurt them again. "You shouldn't have said the problem will be solved by tomorrow."

"Why not?"

"Because some things just can't be solved." She slammed her cup down onto the tray, and cold coffee splashed over the rim. She took a deep breath. Getting mad at Mitch wasn't going to help the situation. She leaned back on the couch, closed her eyes, and started to massage her temples where a headache had started.

Mitch silently watched her, thinking she was wrong. Everything could be solved. He was a scientist working on one of the world's greatest problems—garbage—and how it can be eliminated or recycled. All the answers hadn't been found yet, but between the scientists, industry, and the environmentalists, they were heading in the right direction. One day all the answers would be there. Of course, by then there would be other crises to solve by future scientists. Still, if someone was persistent enough, even the secret of the universe could be unraveled. "Why don't you tell me about it."

Hillary's fingers stilled. She knew what Mitch was asking for—the scandal from her past. She slowly lowered her hands and began to play with the sash on her robe. "Three years ago I was teaching in a Baltimore elementary school. Halfway through the school year one of our regular teachers became ill, and a substitute took over." She took a deep breath and wrapped the end of the sash around her finger. "His name was Bruce Hainley. He was attractive, friendly, and fit right into our school. Everyone liked him. Within a week we were dating." She glanced up and looked at Mitch.

His body was no longer relaxed. He didn't like the idea of Hillary dating another man, even if it had been three years ago. He smiled reassuringly though. "Go ahead."

In a rush she blurted out, "By the end of the month he had moved into my apartment. He had come from Nevada just a few weeks before and had been renting a furnished apartment, so all his stuff was still back home. He flew back there twice to tie up loose ends and visit his parents." She purposely left out any personal feelings. Some things were clearer without mucking them up with emotions. "We went house-hunting together. He wanted a big family home."

Mitch studied the way her fingers were twisting the sash. So far everything she'd said sounded like a fairy tale with happily-ever-after printed at the end. So where was the scandal? "What happened?"

"About a month after Bruce moved in, we had a teachers' meeting one night. The district's elementary teachers were getting together to review the next year's curriculum. We had just started the meeting when a very pregnant woman holding the hand of an eighteen-month-old little boy walked into the room." Hillary gave a halfhearted laugh. "It seemed Bruce had forgotten to mention he already had a wife and family and that he'd abandoned them."

Mitch jumped to his feet and stormed to the large bay window overlooking the street. He jammed his fists into his pockets. He wanted to kill someone. He wanted to wring Bruce's neck.

"There was no way to stop the scandal," she continued, feeling the heated tide of embarrassment flood her cheeks. "It spread like a forest fire throughout the school district and community." Huge tears filled her eyes.

Mitch turned from the window, sat down next to Hillary, and gathered her onto his lap. "If it makes you feel better, go ahead and cry it out for the last time."

Hillary pressed her face into his sweatshirt and tried to stop the tears. All the old memories and doubt came racing back along with this new mess she had gotten herself into. It was all too much for her mind to absorb at once. She snuggled deeper into Mitch's secure embrace and sniffled. It felt wonderful to lean on someone, even for only a minute. Just for this moment everything from the past seemed so insignificant, and the future was a distant blur. There was only the here and now.

Resting his chin on top of her head, Mitch

reached for a tissue from the box on the end table and handed it to her. He waited for her to blow her nose before pulling her back against his chest. She felt soft and feminine nestled up to him, her fragrance all flowery and womanly. He shifted under her and prayed she hadn't noticed his body's response to her sitting on his lap. Now was not the time for raging hormones; there would be plenty of opportunity for that later. First he had to convince her the past didn't matter, and then he had to straighten out this morning's mess.

He stared at her bare leg sticking out from the robe and swallowed. The black stockings the other day hadn't enhanced the long, trim limbs. They were perfectly capable of turning him into a wild creature all on their own. The berry-red toenail polish was the icing on the cake. He wanted that cake. He wanted to know what Hillary was wearing under the soft white robe.

Hillary sighed and breathed in Mitch's essence. He smelled manly with a hint of soap and aftershave. The temptation to stay in his arms for the rest of her life and watch the world go by was overwhelming. She pushed against his chest, slid off his lap to sit beside him, and demurely adjusted the front of the robe. "Thanks for the shoulder."

"Anytime." He turned on the couch to face her. "Who else did this Bruce get over on?"

He made "Bruce" sound like an incurable disease or a slimy creature that lived under a rock. "What do you mean?"

"Who else did he fool? Or did everyone but you know he was married?"

"Good Lord, no. No one had known. His wife's sudden appearance was as much of a shock to everyone who knew him as it was to me."

He lightly held her chin and forced her to meet his eyes. "Did you love him?"

"I . . ."

"Don't answer that. I shouldn't have asked—it's none of my business." Mitch didn't know why he had spoken the question out loud; he already knew the answer. Hillary didn't seem like the type of woman who would invite just anyone to move in with her.

Hillary removed his fingers from her chin and stared down into her lap. After three years it was time to answer that question honestly. "If you mean till-death-do-us-part love, the answer is no. I loved the idea of being in love. I was twenty-eight, alone, and feeling depressed that somehow the world was passing me by. All my friends were married and starting their families. When Bruce entered my life, he was everything I thought I wanted in a man—handsome, charming, and caring. We shared the same interests in teaching, politics, and movies. We never argued. It was perfect, too perfect." She glanced up and met Mitch's gaze. "Do you understand?"

He wrapped an arm around her. "I'm beginning to." He pulled her into the crook of his arm and sat back. "What I don't understand is why you still feel responsible."

"If I hadn't been so damned gullible and naive, it never would have happened."

"That's nonsense, and you know it." He leaned down and locked glances with her. "Bruce was the deceiver, not only to you but everyone else around him He's the guilty party, not you."

"I was the one—"

"No offense, Hillary, but if it hadn't been you, it would have been someone else." He hated to say it, but someone had to. Bruce sounded like a bastard who preyed on other people's weaknesses. Hillary's desire for love and family had been her weakness.

Hillary opened her mouth to object, but no sound emerged. Mitch was right. Bruce's regret the night everything exploded hadn't been at losing Hillary or abandoning his family, it had been at getting caught. How many times had he pulled something similar and not been caught, or how many times since? Images of a young woman with huge, tear-filled brown eyes desperately trying to understand what was going on came back to Hillary. His wife had been in death-do-us-part love with him.

Bruce had been the one who'd crushed that love, not she. And not only had Bruce destroyed his wife's love, but he had also shattered Hillary's trust in men. For three years she had colored all men with the same paintbrush as she had Bruce. Then Mitch came along. There was something trustworthy about him, something that told her she was safe. Could she give in to the growing attraction between them and the warmth he brought to her heart?

A tentative smile touched her lips. "The woman in me says I should take offense at your crack, but I won't. You're right. If it hadn't been me, he would have found someone else."

Mitch mirrored her smile. "Definitely his loss," he said, tenderly brushing a bunch of curls away from her face. "Did I mention how beautiful you look in the morning?"

Hillary tried to gather her wild hair into a fist. It was a hopeless job. Without half a can of mousse her hair looked like something out of *The Twilight Zone*. "My eyes get puffy and red when I cry."

"Don't cry." He lightly traced the freckles dancing across her cheekbones. "Is this where the angels kissed you?"

She rubbed at the offending marks that had caused her hours of misery during her youth. "I thought you were a man of science."

"I am. I know freckles are a small precipitation of pigment in the skin often brought out by the sun." He brushed his lips over the marks. "On you I could believe the angels really did kiss you and left behind their marks."

Hillary closed her eyes. Maybe freckles weren't so bad after all. If Mitch followed her around all day saying such sweet compliments, she might even begin to appreciate the fact that Mother Nature saw fit to bless her with deranged hair. A sparkle of laughter brightened her eyes. Being thankful for a mass of curls that required more time, energy, and skill than a hairstylist from Beverly Hills possessed was ridiculous. "You, sir, are a very dangerous man."

"I aim to please."

She looked away from the warmth glowing in his eyes. In less than an hour he had made her see the scandal for what it was. Not once had he glanced at her with disgust. Years ago her mother had told her that she tended to be harder on herself than other people. It had taken a very special person to make her finally realize that perhaps her mother was right. Mitch was that very special person.

She reached for her cup and froze as her picture glared up at her from the table. How could she have forgotten the paper? Her past might be all tied up in a neat little package in her mind, but this morning's problem wasn't so simple.

Mitch reached for and held her hand. It felt cold and shaky. He was now beginning to understand her fear. If she fought the newspaper, it might bring out the scandal from her past, and Bruce's deception would leave a deeper mark. "I have a couple of things to do this morning. I want you to go back to bed, unplug your phone, and don't answer the door. I'll be back at noon."

"I really don't think that's a good—"

Her protest turned into a sigh of pleasure when he pressed a kiss to her lips. Her arms reached up to encircle his neck, the movement causing the front of her robe to gape open. He slowly released her, and an enticing glimpse of soft, rounded breasts filled his vision. Every male instinct he possessed had reached the same conclusion as his sight. Hillary was naked under the robe.

Wild sparks of heat ignited into burning desire. With his last ounce of willpower he stood up and reached for his jacket. Hillary needed time and space to put the past behind her and to come to grips with having her picture smeared across the checkout counters. What she didn't need, at this point, was the added pressure of a physical relationship. And, boy, did he want to get physical.

Slipping on his jacket, he said in a strained voice, "Trust me on this one."

Hillary brushed a wayward curl out of her eyes. "On what one?" Was he talking about the kiss or the fact that he wanted her to barricade herself in the house until his return?

"You'll see," he promised vaguely. A light kiss landed on the tip of her nose. "I'll be back before lunch. Dress in something old and warm. I promised Ethan I would teach him the old Hail Mary game pass in football."

"What's that got to do with me?"

"You're going to be my receiver." A second kiss brushed her mouth. "I hope you like grilled-cheese sandwiches and tomato soup because that's the Fergusons' standard lunch for cold Sundays. Now behave yourself while I'm gone," he added as he strode out the door.

Hillary sat on the couch in utter amazement. He had done it again. He had waltzed right into her home and taken over her life without so much as a *by-your-leave*. Mitch Ferguson was one of the most arrogant, self-assured males she had ever had the misfortune to run across. Then a wicked smile lit up her face as she thought that he also possessed the sexiest mouth she'd ever had the good luck to kiss. The man was driving her crazy. Half of her wanted to throw him off her property and the other half wanted to ravage his gorgeous body until she stuttered with ecstasy.

With a sigh she picked up the tray of now-cooled coffee and carried it back into the kitchen. She reached into the freezer and pulled out a frozen coffee cake smothered in pecans and oozing white sugary frosting. This morning was definitely a high-cal breakfast morning. She had a feeling she was going to need all the extra energy.

Hillary ran deep, caught the hurling pigskin, and jumped across the broom-handle goal line. With a flourish that would have done Jerry Rice proud, she slammed the football into the ground and wiggled her rear.

Callie giggled, Ethan gave a look of disgust at a female imitating one of his football heroes, and Mitch stopped breathing. Hillary's jean-clad bottom was a vision from his wildest dreams. He had dreamed of that bottom and every other tantalizing inch of Hillary's gorgeous body last night. Witnessing her jubilant display of playfulness was more than his deprived hormones could stand. They wanted to join in on the fun and throw a private celebration of their own with Hillary as the guest of honor.

"You caught it," Callie shouted.

Hillary smiled down at the girl. Callie had leaves clinging to her wind-tossed hair, and her once-clean purple sweatshirt was covered with dirt and grass stains. It was going to take more than a prewash to rediscover the brilliant shade of lavender under all that grime. "Of course I did." With an impish smile she added, "Even though your father can't throw."

Mitch glared at Hillary. "Can't throw!" he yelled, closing the distance between them. "I'll have you know, I went easy on you because I didn't want you to get hurt."

Hillary winked at Callie. "He's just saying that now."

Mitch watched the play between his daughter and Hillary. Callie had finally spoken, and there hadn't been a trace of the baby talk. All through lunch Callie had been noticeably quiet and looked on the verge of tears a couple of times. His heart went out to his daughter and the admirable way Hillary had steered the conversation around Callie so she wasn't forced to answer. Lovely Hillary had scored another direct hit to his heart, and this time her arrow had been his children.

"Throw her another one, Dad," Ethan begged. "And this time throw it *hard*."

Mitch glanced from the confident smile gracing Hillary's lips to the gleam of excitement dancing across his daughter's face. "I have a better idea. How about if we have a little game of touch football?" he said, smiling innocently at Hillary. "You and Callie against me and Ethan."

Hillary saw the devils dancing in his eyes and laughed. He had done it again, offered her a challenge she couldn't back away from. "The sides seem a little unfair . . . considering your advanced age. Are you sure you're up to it?"

With a meaningful glance that encompassed her whole body, he replied, "You'd be surprised at what I could get up for."

Hillary's gaze inadvertently slid to his belt buckle and below as a tide of red swept up her cheeks. The tightening of his jeans attested to the veracity of his statement. She quickly turned from the fascinating view and handed Callie the ball. "Do you want to pass or receive?"

Mitch shifted uncomfortably and berated himself for making the sexual reference. He hadn't meant to embarrass Hillary or make her uncomfortable. Ever since he'd picked her up before lunch, he had acted friendly and nonthreatening. He wanted Hillary to enjoy this afternoon with him and his family and to forget about the newspaper article. By tomorrow the problem would be rectified. Hillary would be receiving a front-page apology from the editor in the morning edition. A satisfied smile came to his lips as he remembered the look on the editor's face when Mitch showed up on his front doorstep on a Sunday morning. The editor and his family had been on their way to church when Mitch very thoroughly explained the situation. He was very proud of himself for mentioning the word "libel" only once during their conversation.

"Hey, Dad, come on!" Ethan hollered.

Mitch broke out of his musing to see Hillary and Callie ready to execute their play. He jogged into position, chuckling at his daughter. Callie was bent over, looking backward between her legs, and seeming ready to hike the ball to Hillary.

"Eighteen, thirty-six, twelve, hike," Hillary shouted. Callie tossed the ball to her left and Hillary made a dive to catch it. Callie dropped back, and Hillary passed the ball back to her, then dashed to block Ethan and keep him from touching his sister.

Laughing, Mitch took after Callie. Hillary had outmaneuvered him. There was no way he would tag his daughter, who was running as fast as her little legs could carry her toward the goal line.

She had rightly guessed that Ethan would have tackled his own grandmother to win a game. So she'd counted on *father's love* to stop Mitch, and it had worked.

Callie crossed the goal line and did a fair imitation of Hillary's rear-twitching victory dance. "I did it, Miss Walker. I did it."

"Yes you did, sweetheart." Hillary smiled apologetically at a frustrated Ethan. "Now it's the guys' turn to try and even up the score."

Ethan's face took on a determined look as he took the ball from his sister. "You pass, Dad. I want to receive."

In a flurry of movements, Ethan broke away from the hiking position and zigzagged across the lawn to catch Mitch's perfectly tossed ball. Hillary started after Ethan only to find her way blocked by a grinning Mitch.

She maneuvered to the left and slammed into a hard chest. "Dammit, Mitch, move."

His hands reached to steady her after the collision. "Not until you say 'pretty please,'" he said, tightening his grip on her hips.

Hillary glanced away from the soft blue plaid flannel shirt covering his chest to Ethan. It was too late. He had already crossed the goal line, with Callie yards behind him. The game was tied. She looked down at Mitch's hands, which still held her intimately. "I thought 'touch football' meant you tag the person with the ball."

"You looked more appealing."

"I could penalize your team ten yards for 'holding.'"

Mitch gave her a squeeze. "It would be worth it." The smooth denim of her jeans felt warm and inviting under his fingertips. How would the graceful curve of her hip feel without the denim barrier? His overactive hormones supplied the answer—silky heat that his hands would just melt over. Before he could lose control, Mitch jammed his trembling hands into the back pockets of his jeans and cursed his adolescent behavior.

"That could be another fifteen yards for a personal foul," Hillary teased.

Mitch quickly glanced over at his children. They were too busy arguing over the tied score to pay attention to two adults. In a lightning-fast movement Mitch leaned forward and placed a quick kiss on Hillary's surprised mouth. "If I'm going to be penalized, I may as well make it worth my while."

Hillary flushed to the roots of her hair, backed away and nervously adjusted the hem of her green-and-black-striped sweater. She was obviously disturbed because he kissed her in front of the children. Hell, he'd made sure the kids weren't even looking.

When Ethan and Callie had learned that Miss Walker would be joining them for lunch, their campaign to get a mother had escalated to new heights. If they had witnessed that harmless kiss, there would be no stopping their excitement. Mitch didn't want his children to be hurt or misled. He wasn't sure where his relationship with Hillary was heading or even if it had a chance to survive. He understood her hesitancy to get romantically involved and could sympathize with any backsliding this morning's newspaper might have caused. Hillary had to come to terms with the past first if she was to find happiness in the future. If he wanted to be part of that future, he had to learn to rein in his desire and develop some patience.

With a heavy sigh he took his position on the field and watched as Callie hiked the ball to Hillary. Instead of passing the ball back to his daughter, Hillary took off down the field in a dead run. Mitch shook off his pondering mode and gave chase.

His long legs ate up the distance between them. Three yards from the goal line he wrapped his arms around her waist and lifted her off her feet.

Hillary was thrown off balance, and Mitch faltered. Within a heartbeat she found herself tumbling to the ground with his arms still around her. She landed on top of his hard body with a resounding thud.

Mitch grunted as the impact of hard dirt and soft, womanly curves assaulted his body. Then he brushed a handful of electric auburn curls from his face and grinned up at the frowning woman clinging to his chest. "Gee, Hillary, I didn't know you cared."

Trying to wiggle out of his arms, she asked, "Are you all right?"

"I won't be if you don't stop wiggling." He tightened his hold as sweat broke out across his brow.

She caught his meaning and stopped struggling immediately. "This was suppose to be *touch* football, not *cream-the-person-with-the-ball*."

Out of the corner of his eye, he saw Callie pick up the ball Hillary had dropped and dash for the goal line. He turned his head and watched as

Ethan gave chase and Callie continued to run around the side of the house, disappearing from sight. Mitch returned his gaze to Hillary's sensual mouth. The lovely pout of her lower lip only made it that much more enticing. He wanted to kiss that pout away. "If you hadn't struggled, we wouldn't have ended up down here."

She tried to loosen his embrace but failed. "It's a fifteen-yard penalty for unnecessary roughness."

Now that they had the entire backyard to themselves, Mitch reached up, cupped the back of Hillary's head and brought her mouth lower. "If I promise to be gentle, would you go easy on me?" he asked, his lips teasing hers.

Thoughts of penalties and football games vanished from her mind as he tenderly coaxed a response from her. She cautiously lifted her head and listened to the far-off shouts of the children. By the sound of their argument it would be some time before they returned to the game. Hillary glanced down into Mitch's eyes. He was allowing her to make the next move. Slowly, she lowered her head and accepted Mitch's warmth.

The sweet, seductive sweep of Hillary's tongue across his lip forced a groan to sound in the back of his throat. Desire was no longer a pleasant adversary; it was a thundering warrior slowly raging out of control. Every ounce of Mitch's willpower was directed to control that desire. He had to remember where they were and his vow to go slowly.

Hillary jerked away from Mitch as the sound of loud throat-clearing penetrated the sensuous fog around them. She noticed a woman leaning against a brightly colored sports car. That the woman had driven it around back and parked it in front of the garage without them hearing it was embarrassing. Hillary jumped off Mitch and stared in amazement at the newcomer.

Whoever she was, she was definitely out of her neighborhood. The young woman looked as if she belonged in the warehouse district of Baltimore and practiced the oldest profession in the world. Platinum-blond hair fell to her waist, and a tight red V-neck sweater attested to the fact that she wasn't wearing a bra and that every overflowing inch of flesh was real. Her black leather miniskirt was tighter across her rear than it had been on the cow, and black fishnet stockings heightened the appearance of her incredibly long legs. The three-inch stiletto heels looked impossible to walk in, much less to prance around in as she flaunted her wares.

Mitch glanced over at his sister and groaned. Why did she have to show up now? She was supposed to have been home around two hours ago, and he had begun to worry about her, but did she really have to appear at this exact moment? "Good morning, Ronnie."

One of her dramatically arched brows rising in response, Veronica Ferguson slowly pushed away from her car and started toward the house. "It's afternoon." She was dead tired from working the streets all night. The ridiculous shoes she had on were killing her feet, but if she'd taken them off, she would have never gotten them back on. The absolute need for a hot shower to wash away the filth of her job, and at least eight hours of sleep, overruled the shock of seeing her older brother lying in the backyard kissing some woman.

Mitch frowned. With the weight of the world seeming to rest on his sister's shoulders, he didn't have to ask how the night had gone. Luck hadn't been with her. He hated what she was doing but understood. Still, every night when she left for work, he worried for her safety and sanity.

Hillary blinked in astonishment as the screen door slammed behind the woman who had just entered Mitch's house. Had she really been wearing earrings the size of small chandeliers and enough makeup to keep a small department store in business for a month? Appalled, she stared at Mitch and asked, "Who was that?"

"My sister, Ronnie."

In horror Hillary stammered, "Your s-sister is a . . ." She couldn't bring herself to say it.

Mitch heard the aversion in Hillary's voice and wondered what had Ronnie done. Then he remembered the way his sister was dressed and started to chuckle. Poor Hillary had jumped to the wrong conclusion. "Ronnie is an undercover policewoman."

Five

"A policewoman?" Hillary asked as she stood up.

"She's on special assignment to the Baltimore Police Department." Mitch rose and brushed off the seat of his jeans. "Sometimes she comes home still dressed in her 'bait' outfits. The kids usually get a kick out of the way she dresses."

"What is she baiting?"

Mitch frowned and pulled a leaf from Hillary's hair. "For the past three weeks she's been trying to attract the attention of a serial killer stalking the prostitutes in the warehouse district."

Hillary stared at Mitch in horror. She could tell by his worried expression that he was serious. His sister dressed like a streetwalker and tried to capture the attention of a killer. "Haven't you tried to persuade her to look for a less dangerous job?"

Mitch gave a wry grin. "Look, Hillary, she's a grown woman, and this is her chosen career." He picked two dead leaves off the back of her sweater.

"Do you let your brother tell you how to live your life?" When he had talked to Matthew this morning, he had seemed concerned at finding his sister's picture plastered on the front page but not neurotically overprotective.

"Of course not. I work with children, teaching them where to place their tongues to make correct sounds. I'm not out there at nights flirting with death." How could he be such a loving father one minute and such an uncaring brother the next?

What did she expect him to do? Lock Ronnie in her room at night? "It's seven nights a week, ten hours at a shot, until 'the Ripper' is caught." The media had christened the killer "the Ripper," because of his preference for prostitutes and the knife, just like Jack the Ripper. An anguished look darkened his expression. The thought of his sister facing such a man in some dark alley froze his blood, no matter how many backups she claimed she had.

Hillary gazed at his tortured expression. By the look on his face, he cared deeply. For one moment she thought she had found some fatal flaw in him, something that would cause her to cease growing more fond of him. She wasn't ready to trust her heart or her instincts yet. They had failed her once. They could do it again. So far Mitch had scored 100 percent on the perfect scale. He was too good to be true.

She tried to ignore the little voice in her head that screamed if he was too good to be true, he probably was—but couldn't. The voice was growing louder with each second. Mitch could either be the man of her dreams or the nemesis from her worst nightmare. The probability of Mitch having a wife stashed somewhere was nil, but there were other sins. He could be an enemy spy, or an ex-member of the mob hiding out on the witness-protection program, or Lord forbid, an ex-used car salesman. His sister had seemed unconcerned at finding him locked in a heated embrace in the middle of the backyard with some stranger. Either she was so tired that it didn't even register in her mind or Mitch frolicked in the grass with amazing regularity.

What *did* she know about Mitch? Absolutely nothing about his past, which was the same thing she knew about his future, or even his present. Mitch Ferguson was an iceberg. She knew only about the one tenth that was above water. The remaining nine tenths were still a mystery

Everyone, from Eunice to the children, had made her feel welcome today. Finding herself in the bosom of Mitch's family was disturbing. It was all too perfect. The big house, two loving children, and a gorgeous single man. She could step right in, make herself at home, and complete the fantasy life she had always dreamed of having. The appeal was great. She had to get away and put some distance between them before the temptation became a reality. "Maybe you should take me home now."

"Why?"

"Your sister needs her sleep, and Eunice is busy covering the living room furniture with drop cloths. Company is the last thing they need."

"Ronnie has the entire third floor to herself, and Eunice has been covering furniture since we moved here three months ago. Company wouldn't faze them one way or another." He didn't want her to leave. This afternoon was one of the most pleasant he had spent in a long time. He thought she was enjoying herself too. So why did she want to go home? The afternoon was barely half over.

Ethan and Callie came dashing around the house just then, with Ethan carrying the ball and Callie dead on his heels trying to get it back. The antics of the children had helped take Hillary's mind off this morning's newspaper, but reality was starting to rear its ugly head. She had to come to terms with the article and figure out what to do about it, if anything.

"It was nice of you to invite me over," she told Mitch. "I really enjoyed myself."

"How about staying for dinner? I'm not sure what we're having, but Eunice filled the Crockpot with something great smelling this morning."

"It sounds tempting, but I really ought to be heading home."

Mitch tried another tactic. "The kids would love to have you stay." He glanced at his children and saw Ethan dash behind a bush. Callie let out a bloodcurling scream of defeat; she almost had him that time. With the two acting unruly, Mitch couldn't blame Hillary if she refused.

"They are sweet, but I have a million things at home that have to be done."

Mitch stepped in closer and gently tilted up her chin. Her eyes held a wistful look in their depths.

His thumb stroking her full bottom lip, he whispered, "I would love to have you stay."

Hillary sighed in defeat. Mitch had just offered her the greatest temptation of all: himself. How could she ignore that?

He read the indecision in her eyes and added a further incentive. "I'll even give you a tour of my lab." He wiggled his eyebrows like Groucho Marx and jerked his head toward the garage.

Amused by how easily he had swayed her mind, she chuckled. "Is this the same thing as showing someone your etchings?"

"I can't even doodle well, but I do own a great collection of posters."

"The pinup kind?"

"Of course. All my posters are pinned up." He took her hand and started toward the garage.

After Ethan and Callie were excused from the dinner table, they huddled together in her bedroom. He pulled the crinkled piece of paper from his pocket and smiled. Miss Walker had just scored another mark in her favor. She, too, had made a face at the broccoli. For the first time that he could remember, their father hadn't made them eat their vegetables, and Hillary was responsible. "Look, Callie, Miss Walker didn't eat her vegetables." His finger pointed to number 3 on the list.

Callie frowned. She didn't care about broccoli or any other vegetables. She was more interested to know if Hillary could bake fancy cupcakes and allowed sleepovers. She was going to turn eight on her next birthday; surely that was old enough for her first sleepover. "So?"

She watched as her brother drew a big red *X* through the number 3. "We only have four things crossed off. How are we going to find out about the other six?"

Ethan carefully refolded the tattered clipping and placed it in his back pocket. "We just have to make sure we're always around Miss Walker and Dad. The more we're with her, the easier it will be." He headed for the closed door. "Come on, let's get back downstairs and see what else we can find out."

Today was the day Callie had promised her Barbie a pool party. With a resigned sigh and a backward glance at her collection of dolls, she followed Ethan. Getting a mother was proving to be a tougher job than she had first thought.

"Can we come too, Dad?"

Mitch looked at Ethan and tried to hide his scowl. He was ready to take Hillary home and was looking forward to spending some time alone with her. The last thing he wanted was his own children tagging along. What kind of father did that make him? He glanced over at Hillary, following the elegant curve of her jaw and sexy swell of her lower lip with his gaze, and knew the answer. It made him a very human kind of father.

"Shouldn't you be starting on your homework?" he asked the kids.

"I've already done it," Ethan answered.

"I don't have any, Dad," Callie added.

"What about your reading?" He was starting to feel desperate.

"Aunt Ronnie read us our library books yesterday."

"Let them come, Mitch," Hillary said, smiling encouragingly at the kids. "It'll take only a few minutes to run me home." If Mitch drove her back alone, she knew she would end up either in bed with him or frustrated again. She was too old to be taking cold showers that never helped, but she wasn't sure if she was ready for the alternative.

It was three against one. Mitch knew a losing battle when he saw one. "All right, kids, get your coats on." He frowned as a look of relief washed over Hillary's face. So much for any heated good-night kisses.

Hillary slowly made her way down the empty school hall. The thought of showing up for work this morning had kept her up all night. Everyone had to have seen yesterday's paper. Only a blind person wouldn't have recognized her from the picture on the front page. She resigned herself to a day of sly looks and snide remarks.

For hours last night she had stared at the photo, trying to decide what was the best way to handle it. Her usually fertile mind had drawn a blank. She wanted a retraction. She wanted a written apology. Hell, what she really wanted was someone's head on a silver platter. How dare they take her picture without her consent, and then plaster it on the front page for all the world to see! The final insult had been their not even getting her name or occupation right. Maybe Mitch was right about suing for libel and damn the consequences. Bruce was the sludge of the earth, and she was tired of running from sludge.

Some people were wave-makers in the pool of life. It came as quite a surprise to realize she was a treader. Even with all her independence and self-reliance she was still a treader. She lacked the nerve to confront the newspaper and demand some form of retraction. Anyone would think a person living in a town called Oz would acquire some courage like the Cowardly Lion. But then again, this Oz didn't have a Wizard.

Hillary opened the door to the teachers' lounge and forced a smile at two of her colleagues. "Good morning, Ed, Donna."

Ed refolded the newspaper he had been reading. "Who in the hell do you know in such high places?"

The color slowly seeped out of Hillary's face. "What do you mean?"

Donna waved Sunday's early edition under her nose. "Let me tell you, I was extremely jealous of you. Imagine going out with a congressman."

Appalled, Hillary said, "I wasn't out with him!"

"I know that now, but yesterday I didn't. The only thing I couldn't figure out was why they called you Bambi."

"You mean, you didn't believe I was an exotic dancer from the Paradise Club?" Hillary asked sarcastically. How could Donna be so small-minded as to actually think she would date such a lecherous man? Bruce might have been sludge at the bottom of the lake, but the congressman was pond scum. He floated on top for all the world to see.

"Heavens, no. Really, Hillary. A person must possess a certain amount of"—she glanced meaningfully at Hillary's chest—"you know what, to be one of those dancers."

Hillary was beginning to see red. There was nothing wrong with her chest size. She didn't need American Bridge to design her support system, but then again her sweaters didn't bag where they weren't supposed to.

"There's nothing wrong with Hillary's . . ." Ed's words trailed off when both women turned on him. "I mean . . . if Hillary wanted to be some topless dancer, she wouldn't starve." Panic flashed in his eyes as Hillary advanced. "I meant it as a compliment."

Hillary wasn't sure if she wanted to laugh or cry. The look on Ed's face was priceless; his third graders would get a kick out of seeing his distress. Strangling Ed might relieve some of her tension, but it wouldn't solve her problems, just add to them. With a weary sigh she headed to the coffeepot. "Believe what you want, but I was accidentally pushed onto the congressman's lap. I never even met the man. The photographer happened to snap that picture at the worse possible moment."

"We know that."

Hillary stopped in her tracks and turned around. "What do you mean, you know that?"

How could anyone who wasn't at the Ruby Slipper know that?

Ed held up the morning paper. "The whole state knows it by now."

She grabbed the paper and scanned the headlines. This morning she had picked up her newspaper from the front porch without even glancing at it and threw it in the bottom of her kitchen wastebasket. She had made up her mind to cancel her subscription. Any newspaper that didn't bother to check its facts wasn't worth reading.

Her heart skipped a beat as bold black letters captured her attention. There on the bottom of the front page was the caption: *Please Accept Our Apologies*. The article went on to explain the error in yesterday's newspaper. Hillary was never mentioned by name, but it went on to reveal how an innocent bystander was pushed onto the congressman's lap just as the photographer snapped his picture. Both the editor and the photographer apologized for the misunderstanding and hoped there would be no hard feelings or repercussions from the innocent bystander.

Hillary was in shock. They had apologized, and on the front page, no less. In her secret fantasies she visualized the written apology to appear on page 47. Right under the obituary column.

"You didn't know about this article, did you?" Ed asked.

"I hadn't a clue." She handed Ed back his paper, feeling victorious. They had humbly apologized. It didn't quite make up for the injustice of it all, but it was more than she expected.

"What did you threaten them with? Libel? Defamation of character?" Donna asked.

"Nothing." A frown wiped away Hillary's pleased expression. "I didn't even notify them of their mistake."

Ed looked over the article again. "Someone had to have said something, Hillary."

Hillary stared out the window, too deep in thought to take in the beautiful fall colors of the trees in the empty playground. Someone *had* said something, and that someone had to have been Mitch. That was what was so important yesterday morning. Now she understood his pleased expression when he had picked her up for lunch and the football game. Mitch had confronted the editor and demanded the apology on her behalf. He had gone out and fought her battle for her. Damn his chauvinistic hide. She didn't want him, or anyone else, slaying her dragons. They were *her* dragons, by hell! If anyone was to confront the beast, it should have been her.

"Hillary?"

She turned and glanced at a concerned-looking Donna. "Hey, look at the time. I have to be going." Her footsteps weren't as light as they normally were as she headed for the door.

Three other teachers came strolling in just then. "Well, lookie here. If it ain't Bambi for-a-day," joked a tall, willowy woman.

"Shhh! Barbara. You knew Hillary wasn't out with that political scum even before this morning's paper," snapped Blanche, the elderly woman beside her.

"I was only teasing, Hillary," Barbara said.

Everyone was being seminice about the picture. No one had ever accused her of not having a sense of humor. Maybe she should just laugh it off and chalk it up as another experience of life. "I know, Barb."

Barbara grinned. "The real issue here is not the picture of you and the Capitol Cretin." She leaned in closer but didn't lower her voice. "What I want to know is, who *were* you with at the Ruby Slipper Saturday night?"

A flood of red stained her face as she opened the door. "Obviously someone I shouldn't have gone out with." Hillary kept her head high as she walked down the hall to her classroom.

Blanche chuckled. "I know who she was with."

Four sets of eyes turned on her. "Who?"

"You young pups really ought to attend our football games on Friday nights. You'd be surprised at some of the sights you could see in that old stadium." She was still chuckling as she waltzed out the door.

Hillary glared at the man standing on her porch. "Well, if it isn't Mr. Dragon Slayer."

Mitch was so startled by the hostility in her voice, he looked behind him to make sure no one else was standing there. He had no idea what she was talking about, but her irate tone spoke of ill will. Tonight wasn't going to go as he had planned. "You lost me somewhere."

She leaned against the jamb and barred him from entering the house. "Wishful thinking on my part." The more she thought about what he had done, the madder she had gotten. What right did he have to go to the newspaper and demand an apology? It wasn't *his* reputation being questioned.

"You're upset about something."

"Give the man a prize."

Mitch had expected Hillary to welcome him warmly with a word of thanks. He wasn't after her gratitude, but right now a kind word wouldn't go amiss. Frustrated and confused, he ran his fingers through his hair. The cause of Hillary's distress had to be the retraction in this morning's newspaper, but why? Whatever the reason, he had a feeling he was about to find out what kind of temper his redheaded lady possessed. "How about inviting me in for a cup of coffee? It's cold out here."

Hillary took in his stubborn stance and sighed. Mitch didn't look as if he were going to move off her porch until he was good and ready. He didn't look ready, and she couldn't stand here all night with the front door open. She moved away from the door and walked into the living room. "It has to be a quick cup. I'm very busy."

He closed the door behind him and took off his jacket before following Hillary into the kitchen. "I gather you've seen this morning's paper."

She slammed the teakettle on the back burner and jerked the knob to the on position. "Whatever gave you that idea?"

Mitch studied her body language. He was a dead man. "You didn't want the newspaper to apologize?"

"Of course I did."

Now he was totally confused. "Then why are you so upset?"

The ceramic coffee cups were in danger of breaking as she banged them onto the counter and glared at the man standing in front of her. "I'll tell you why I'm so upset." She placed her hands on her hips and snapped, "Because you went to them and demanded it, didn't you?"

"What else was I supposed to do?"

"You were supposed to allow me to handle it. After all, it was my problem."

"You said you weren't going to do anything." He slowly sank down on a stool. "I thought you would be pleased."

"Pleased! No one asked you to go fighting my battles for me."

"You expected me to sit back and allow you to be hurt?" He shook his head sadly. "I admit that I'm a little rusty at dating and building a relationship. It's been seventeen years since I dated anyone besides Ethan and Callie's mother, Catherine. Has it changed that much?"

"Haven't you heard of ERA?"

"I'm all for equal rights. Haven't you ever heard of a gentleman?"

"A gentleman doesn't put his nose in where it doesn't belong." She yanked the whistling kettle off the burner and poured the water into the cups. "I'm not some poor helpless female."

"I never thought you were."

"Then why did you do it?" She couldn't prevent herself from asking the fifty-thousand-dollar question. "Was it out of pity?" All day long she couldn't help thinking that Mitch had rushed to her rescue because of what had happened in her past. Having been played for a fool was one thing, but having a very attractive man think she still was one was too humiliating—and infuriating.

"Pity?" Mitch burst out laughing. Someone had completely misunderstood the situation. He wasn't sure anymore if it was Hillary or him.

Her hand tightened on the sugar bowl. If it wouldn't make such a mess, she'd chuck it at his head. How dare he laugh!

Mitch watched Hillary in utter amazement. He could actually see her temper rise. Curbing the urge to grin, he stood up and cautiously made his way around the counter. He carefully took the sugar bowl out of her hand and placed it on the counter. "The only person I pity is me."

Her green eyes lost their hardness, and her mouth relaxed as Mitch cupped her cheeks and forced her to look up at him.

"There were a lot of reasons to go and insist the paper retract the story. The first thing it was untrue." He leaned against the refrigerator and pulled Hillary against his chest. "You wouldn't have been at the Ruby Slipper that night if it weren't for me." He brushed back a wayward curl and lightly traced the delicate curve of her ear. His finger played with the dangling silver earring, sending it gently swaying. "But the real reason I went pounding on the editor's door was because that story had hurt you."

Hillary swallowed hard. Where had all her anger gone? It had taken her all day to build up a nice head of steam. It had taken Mitch less than five

Thanks for reading LOVESWEPT!

Now, enter our

Winners Classic
SWEEPSTAKES
and go for the
Vacation Of Your Dreams!

Here's your chance to win a *fabulous* 14-day holiday for two in romantic Hawaii ... exciting Europe ... or the sizzling Caribbean! Use one of these stickers to tell us your choice — and ***go for it!***

Plus — $5,000.⁰⁰ CASH!

Send Me To **HAWAII**

Send Me To **EUROPE**

Send Me To The **CARIBBEAN**

Send My **FREE GIFTS!**

FREE GIFTS, TOO!

Six scintillating Loveswept romance novels *and* this terrific makeup case — complete with lighted mirror — are YOURS FREE!

NO COST OR OBLIGATION TO BUY
See details inside ...

Ah, Romance...

Don't you just *love* being in love? And what could be more romantic than you and your special someone sunning on the beach in exotic Hawaii, holding hands, listening to the pounding surf ... or strolling arm and arm around London, hearing Big Ben strike midnight as you toast each other with champagne ... or slipping out of a casino to walk along the silky beaches of the Caribbean on a warm, moonlit night? Sounds wonderful, doesn't it?

WIN A ROMANTIC INTERLUDE AND $5,000.00 CASH!

What's even *more* wonderful is that **you could win** one of these romantic **14-day vacations for two**, plus **$5,000.00 CASH**, in the Winners Classic Sweepstakes! To enter, just affix the vacation sticker of your choice to your Official Entry Form and drop it in the mail. It costs you nothing to enter (we even pay postage!) — so *go for it!*

FREE GIFTS!

We've got **six FREE Loveswept Romances** and a **FREE Lighted Makeup Case** ready to send you, too!

If you affix the **FREE GIFTS** sticker to your Entry Form, your first shipment of Loveswept Romances is yours absolutely FREE. Plus, about once a month, you'll get six *new* books hot off the presses, *before they're available in bookstores*. You'll always have 15 days to decide whether to keep any shipment, for our low regular price, currently just $13.50* — that's 6 books for the price of five! **You are never obligated to keep any shipment**, and may cancel at any time by writing "cancel" across our invoice and returning the shipment to us, at our expense. There's **no risk** and **no obligation** to buy, *ever*.

Now that's a pretty sweet offer, I think you'll agree — but we've made it even sweeter! We'll also send you the **Lighted Makeup Case** shown on the other side of this card — **absolutely FREE!** It has an elegant tortoise-shell finish, and comes with an assortment of brushes for eye shadow, blush and lip color. And the lighted mirror makes sure your look is always *perfect!*

BOTH GIFTS ARE ABSOLUTELY FREE AND ARE YOURS TO KEEP FOREVER, no matter what you decide about future shipments! So come on! You risk nothing at all — and you stand to gain a world of sizzling romance, exciting prizes ... and FREE GIFTS!

*(plus shipping & handling, and sales tax in NY and Canada)

ENTER NOW TO WIN A FABULOUS VACATION <u>AND</u> $5,000.00 CASH! GET <u>FREE</u> BOOKS <u>AND</u> A <u>FREE</u> LIGHTED MAKEUP CASE!

NO COST • NO RISK • NO OBLIGATION TO BUY

Winners Classic
SWEEPSTAKES
OFFICIAL ENTRY FORM

Don't miss out! It's **FREE** to
enter our sweepstakes ... the first six books are
FREE ... and the lighted makeup case is **FREE!**
You have nothing to lose — so enter today.

Good luck.

minutes to kill it. "You still shouldn't have done it."

He read the softening in her eyes. Her fingers weren't clenched into fists against his chest any longer; they were gently caressing the front of his sweater. "I'm sorry for upsetting you. The next time I'll get your permission before I start threatening libel suits."

She groaned and pressed her forehead against his chest. "You didn't."

"Sure I did. And it worked," he said, pulling her closer.

The urge to laugh combated her desire to cry. He had gone and done what she didn't have the courage to do. She would have loved to have seen the look on the editor's face when Mitch started spouting threats of libel suits and court appearances.

Mitch felt the gentle shaking of her shoulders and didn't know if she was laughing or crying. He tipped up her chin and relaxed when her soft chuckle floated upward. "Am I forgiven?"

Hillary gazed up into his honest brown eyes. He had jumped to her rescue out of some instinct to protect her, not because he had felt sorry for her. It was a sweet, misguided gesture. "Maybe." Then remembering what he'd said earlier, she murmured, "You never explained why you pitied yourself."

"My entire world has been turned upside down since I've met you."

She liked the way his eyes turned all hot and smoldering. The man could melt steel ingots with that look. "Aren't you afraid you'll fall off?"

Mitch watched her lips with a feverish fascination. Hillary Walker was either going to be the death of him, or his life. He pulled her closer until the fullness of her breasts was pressed into his chest and the seductive curves of her thighs was cradled between his legs. He lowered his mouth to her waiting lips. "Oh, I'm falling, all right."

Six

Hillary sighed in satisfaction as Mitch's mouth settled firmly over hers. The heat of his mouth and his hands melted away any lingering doubts she still might have harbored. Waves of pleasure washed over her as his tongue swept boldly past her lips to lay claim to the hidden treasure within. Desire sparked, then quickly ignited. She wrapped her arms around his neck and tried to get closer to the flame.

Strong hands cupped her jean-covered rear and pulled her snugly against his arousal. Nights of frustration were straining against the zipper of his jeans.

A shiver of excitement slipped down her spine as warm fingers slid under her oversized sweatshirt to lightly stroke her back. The need to touch Mitch in the same way burned at her fingertips. Wanting to feel his strength and texture, she yanked at the hem of his sweater and slipped it up his shirt-covered back. He broke the kiss, pulled the sweater over his head, and tossed it to the floor.

Hillary's fingers immediately went to the row of buttons on his shirt. She grinned as Mitch picked her up and sat her on the counter. "Eunice would have a fit if she saw the way you treated your clothes."

Her impatient hands pushed his unbuttoned shirt off his shoulders until it fell, landing on top of the sweater. Lovingly, her fingers caressed the sleek smoothness of his shoulders, the subtle bulges gracing his arms.

"Then it's a good thing she's not here," he said, his strong, masculine hands spanning her trim waist. He watched, enthralled, as she stroked his chest and wove through the dense curls. He couldn't picture a more exotic sight then her pale peach-tipped fingers buried beneath the dark curls. Molten heat radiated from his every pore as his hands slowly moved up her stomach to cup her breasts and his thumb gently followed the intriguing outline of her midnight-blue satin and lace bra.

"Hillary, open your eyes." He wanted to see the desire there. He needed to know that she was just as affected by his touch as he was by hers.

Hillary obeyed the whispered command and was rewarded by the multitude of delicious sins reflected in his gaze. She wanted to experience every one of those sins. Nearly trembling from excitement, she pulled her sweatshirt over her head and dropped it on the growing pile.

Oxygen was a luxury Mitch's poor body forgot to take in as he gazed at Hillary. She was beautiful.

Her breasts were firm and full. Her green eyes were glazed with passion, and auburn curls tumbled down her back in wild disarray. Her lips, which were puffy and red from his kisses, seemed to be begging for more. He gently spread her knees apart and settled himself more firmly between her thighs. Denim rubbed against denim. Satin and lace rubbed against his heated chest. "Lord, you are perfect."

Her eager hands slipped up his chest, then around his neck. "Hardly," she answered, pulling his mouth closer, playfully nibbling on his lower lip. She felt him shiver and heard a rough groan as her tongue teased a corner of his mouth. Tonight Mitch would be staying. It was written in the trembling of his fingers and quickness of his breath as he undid the front clasp of her bra and slid the garment off her shoulders.

He cupped her full white breasts, gazing at twin pink nipples that poked through his fingers and pouted for attention. A grin of pure male satisfaction spread across his face as the nubs hardened into ripe little berries. With immense care he bent down, tasted the erotic morsels, and filled his mouth with the sweet essence of Hillary.

Hillary's fingers clutched at his hair while desire and need flowed like molten steel to the juncture of her thighs. She could feel the evidence of his need straining his jeans and rocking against her rhythmically. She wanted to *dance* to that rhythm. She wanted Mitch.

A shudder of excitement caused her to stutter as she declared her desire with one word, "S-s-stay."

Mitch reluctantly raised his head and grinned. Hillary stuttered when she was aroused. It was an appealing trait, one that was a turn-on. Wondering just how far her stuttering would go, he slipped his hands under her thighs and picked her up. "Oh, lady, try keeping me away now."

Hillary wrapped her arms and legs around him. Three years of self-discipline had disappeared under Mitch's tender ministrations. Her wayward mouth had forgotten how to speak. She pressed her face into his neck and tightened her hold as Mitch carried her out of the kitchen and down the hall to the bedroom.

A pale shaft of light from the street lamp outside cast a sensual glow over the room. Mitch walked over to the huge white iron bed and slowly lowered Hillary to her feet. His fingers toyed with the snap on her jeans. "Are you sure?"

Her fingers played with the snap on his jeans. "Positive." She was absolutely sure about going to bed with Mitch. It was the rest of her life she was uncertain about. She wasn't ready for commitments and promises, and Mitch wasn't offering any. Tonight all she wanted was satisfaction in his arms, nothing more and nothing less.

With a flick of her fingers the snap came undone. Then she lowered his zipper, the sound echoing loudly in the silent room. Mitch grabbed her hands and pulled them to his chest. "Oh, lady, you are dangerous."

Hillary found a dark nipple peeking out from under a patch of brown curls. She licked the sensitive bud and grinned as it swiftly turned into a hardened pebble. "Wait, you haven't seen anything yet," she said, though she had no idea what she was going to do that could be considered dangerous. For the first time in her life she felt really desirable and wanted to return the experience. This wasn't going to be just sex, it was going to be pure pleasure.

With a quick jerk Mitch turned down the quilt and top sheet, then took off her jeans and peeled the tiny scrap of midnight-blue panties down her long legs. He sucked in a harsh breath. She looked like a goddess standing naked and proud in the shaft of pale light. With impatient hands he rapidly shed the rest of his clothes and pulled her into his arms.

His chest was solid and unyielding, and his arms felt like bands of steel. Strong thighs trembled against the sleek smoothness of hers as he plunged his tongue past her lips. His maleness, the essence of his desire, was hard and throbbed against her abdomen.

His iron control started to slip as small, delicate hands slid down his back to gently squeeze his rear. Without breaking the kiss, he tightened his hold on Hillary and fell backward onto the bed, bringing her with him. A rough groan emerged from his throat as Hillary squirmed on top of him.

She captured his groan with her mouth and caressed the tempting curve of his hipbone with her fingertips. She could feel the quivering of his arousal as it pressed against the downy curtain of curls covering her womanhood.

Mitch broke the kiss and rolled over, pinning her under him. His control had reached its limits. "Tell me you're ready, Hillary," he demanded softly, his fingers combing through the downy curls. He felt her wetness and knew she was ready for him, but he wanted to hear her say it.

Hillary arched her back and thrust her hips out farther as a finger slowly slipped into her. "M-M-Mit . . ." She shook her head in defeat. Her mouth refused to work. Lord, couldn't he feel she was ready?

Her stuttering was about to send him over the edge. The knowledge that he excited her to the point where she couldn't talk was a powerful aphrodisiac. He gently positioned himself between her thighs and gazed down into her face. Lord, she was beautiful when aroused. Her cheeks were flushed, and her untamed hair was spread out across the pale sheets like wildfire.

When he gently nudged the opening, Hillary urged him on by wrapping her legs around his hips. He slowly entered the tight moistness, and the silky heat had him shuddering and his control snapping. With wild abandonment he started their journey toward the summit. He wasn't going over the edge without taking Hillary with him.

Desire riding through her like a runaway train, she matched Mitch thrust for thrust. Speed and excitement built to a mind-shattering numbness. Both strained toward the completion of their journey. Both wanted the voyage to last a lifetime.

Hillary felt the end approaching fast and tried to hold back. She didn't want the wild train ride to stop. Gasping for breath, she tried to slow down, tried to prolong the inevitable.

Mitch felt her hesitancy and increased the rhythm. He couldn't last much longer; Hillary was sending him over the edge. He begged her to join him: "Hillary, now!" He felt the violent shuddering that signaled her climax, and with a final thrust joined her.

Ten minutes went by before Mitch could gather up all his senses and ask, "Are you all right?"

Hillary raised her head from his chest. "Couldn't be better." She was pressed against his side and wrapped snugly in his embrace. One of them, she wasn't sure which, had pulled the quilt up for added warmth. As if they needed it after the inferno of their lovemaking! She nestled deeper into his embrace and grinned. So this was heaven!

His arms tightened around her. They couldn't get any closer unless he was in her, he thought, then felt his body's natural response to the image. *So much for control.*

Hillary's smile widened as his body hardened. The man was amazing, but more important, the man was in her bed. She lightly trailed her fingers up a hair-roughened thigh.

Mitch groaned in frustration when her teasing fingers stopped a few inches away from his straining manhood. "You're playing with fire."

She drew a circle in the thick patch of curls ringing his arousal. "Then it's a good thing I'm not a scarecrow."

"Scarecrow?" What was she talking about? His mind slipped into another gear as her fingers inched closer. He wanted to feel the warmth of her palm surrounding him, but he forced himself not to turn toward the tempting hand.

A gentle kiss brushed his chest. "Don't you remember where you live?"

With her hands and lips caressing his body, he'd forgotten his own name. "We live in Oz." He was rewarded with another sweet kiss. "The scarecrow was afraid of fire." He sucked in air as her hand encircled his arousal.

From its velvety tip to its rigid base, heat and power emanated from beneath its satiny surface. Moving her hand slowly up and down its length, she asked, "If you really were in the Land of Oz, which character would you be?"

Mitch raised his hips, trying to increase her torturously slow rhythm. "The Mayor of Munchkin Land," he answered, naming his favorite character.

Hillary chuckled, said, "I think not," then lightly squeezed the portion of his anatomy that proved her point. There was nothing little about Mitch.

He rolled over, pulling her beneath him. It was his turn to play the game. He bent his head to capture one of her hardened nipples between his lips and playfully drew it into his mouth, bathing it with his tongue.

She moaned, arched her hips, and tried to entice him into her warmth. The first wild train ride had only whetted her appetite for more. She needed Mitch to take her there again.

His mouth nuzzled the smoothness of her stomach. He wanted to hear her stutter again. "What character would you be?" he asked, his warm breath teasing the thatch of tight auburn curls.

Her hands clutched at the sheet. "The Wicked W-W-Wit-Witch of the W-W-W . . ." Frustration made her grip the sheet harder. She felt she was melting, and water hadn't even been thrown on her. With determination she uttered the last word: "West!"

Mitch smiled into the curls. Hillary could never be a witch. An angel possibly, but never a witch. "I think not."

Hillary grabbed the bar of soap and lathered her body. She had very interesting whisker burns in the most unusual places. Muscles that hadn't been used in a long time relaxed under the steaming spray. She wished she had some more time to spend under the shower, but if she didn't get a move-on, she was going to be late for work. With a reluctant sigh she turned off the water and reached for a towel.

A frown pulled at the corner of her mouth as scenes from last night played across her mind. What Mitch and she had shared went beyond sex. There had been a special spark, a moment of magic, when they had made love. Desires and feelings never experienced before had stormed her senses, begging to be explored.

Hillary had slammed the door against those feelings. She didn't want any messy emotions cluttering up her relationship with Mitch. She didn't want to open the door and face feelings better left tucked away in the dark. If she didn't acknowledge any tender emotions, then she wouldn't be vulnerable to Mitch.

She stepped out of the bathroom and prepared for work, her fingers rougher than usual as she pinned her hair into a bun. After straightening the high lace collar at her throat and pulling on a navy-blue blazer, she glanced at herself in the mirror. She looked neat and professional. No one looking at her would see the passionate woman from last night.

The relationship she was having with Mitch was perfect. No promises, no pledges of undying love, and no commitments. No one would get hurt. Her heart couldn't be broken if it wasn't involved. She was safe as long as she kept the door to her soul locked tightly.

Her steps were purposeful as she picked up her purse and left the house. She was a woman of the nineties. She wasn't going to allow her past to taint what she had with Mitch. This relationship was going to be straightforward and honest.

But after putting the key in the ignition, she lowered her forehead to the cold, hard plastic of the steering wheel. She had already blown the honesty part. She had lied to Mitch. She wasn't the Wicked Witch of the West, she was more like the Cowardly Lion.

Mitch leaned farther back in the chair. His feet were propped up on the pile of magazines and reports cluttering his desk, and his hands were clasped behind his head. His deep, off-key voice filled the lab as he sang along with a Bob Dylan classic blaring from the radio. He felt eighteen again, with the whole world in front of him. He was in love.

He stared up at the ceiling and grinned like an idiot. He had never thought it would happen twice in his lifetime. His love for Catherine had been perfect and true, but it was in the past. It was time to face the future—and his future contained one very passionate speech pathologist named Hillary Walker.

His fingers lightly touched the nick under his chin, and he winced. He had been in the middle of shaving this morning when it had hit him. He had fallen in love with Hillary. He wasn't sure exactly when, or even why, but the fact remained, he had fallen. That she stuttered when she was excited was endearing, but surely that wasn't the reason he fell. She was smart, compassionate, and funny, and her kisses were dynamite. It wasn't one thing that made Hillary unique, it was the entire package.

For five years everyone from his sister to his parents had been worried about his lack of interest in dating again. In the back of his mind even he had started to question his lack of desire. But that was before Hillary. One afternoon with her, and his hormones had become raging maniacs. His body had known what his heart had just discovered: Hillary was the one. She was the woman he had been waiting for all those years, and it had taken his children to find her.

Ethan and Callie were going to be thrilled when they learned their plan had worked. They were going to get a mother.

Mitch glanced around the lab without really seeing the beakers, Bunsen burners, or the crates of equipment Greenleaves had delivered last week. He wondered if Hillary would mind becoming an instant mother to his kids. Ethan and Callie were the two most perfect children on this earth, even if they were a handful at times. Hillary had seemed to get along with them the other day, but a two-hour football game was a far cry from living with them. Being a teacher didn't automatically mean Hillary had an overabundance of maternal desires.

Which left another interesting question: How would his children react to finally getting their wish? Praying, pleading, and begging for a mother was entirely different from actually having one. It was the same situation as kids seeing those exciting toy commercials on television two months before Christmas. They would beg Santa to bring them the latest craze, and then they were mightily disappointed when they opened the package and saw how different the toy was from the advertisement. A mother couldn't be returned to the store for a full refund.

The grin slowly faded from Mitch's face. This was going to be a lot harder than he had anticipated. Not only was he unsure of Hillary's reaction, but he had to consider Ethan and Callie. And what about Eunice? She had been a part of the family since Ethan was six weeks old. For the past five years she ran the household with love on one hand and a paintbrush in the other. Eunice painted rooms the way most people changed their underwear. What would happen if Hillary should be allergic to paint fumes? Ronnie moving in hadn't been a threat to Eunice's domain. Ronnie was the most undomesticated female ever to wear high heels. Half the time Mitch thought Ronnie's insistence on providing a female influence for his children was only an excuse to having Eunice cook her meals and do the laundry.

If, or more accurately when, Hillary became his wife, he would have three females living under his roof. His gaze settling on the poster of the periodic table, he wondered which element best described each female. Whatever they were, he prayed they were compatible when mixed. Explosions could kill a man, or at least make him go prematurely gray.

"I need to borrow the car, Mitch."

He jerked in surprise and spun around toward the door. Eunice was standing in the middle of the lab frowning at the unpainted walls. He hadn't heard her come in. "Sure, what for?" It was a silly question considering what she was wearing. Her old sweatshirt was dotted and smeared with so many different shades of paint, he had no idea which color she was currently using. This morning he had only half listened to her as she told him something about the dining room. Obviously it had been the next room on her list.

"The stupid bozo from the paint store didn't mix the paint right. I asked for Serenity Green."

He reached into his pocket for his keys. "What did you get?"

"Right now the one wall in the dining room looks like there's algae growing on it." She walked over to a wall and ran her hand over the Sheetrock and spackle. "This needs to be sanded before I can paint it."

Mitch tossed her the keys. Facing algae while eating sounded about as appealing as eating it. "I told you that I don't have time to paint." He purposely had hung up posters to cover the bare walls, which, to Eunice, were like a red flag to a bull. She would come charging in here with rollers, primers, sandpaper, and stepladders. If he was lucky, she would try only four or five different colors before being satisfied.

She ignored him and continued to study the walls. "It might take two coats of primer before I could paint." She moved a cardboard box and frowned. "They did a lousy spackle job. I'm going to have to touch it up." She put the box back and glanced around the large room. The only light came from two small windows and an overhead fixture Mitch had installed. "I think I'll use a pale yellow to brighten up the place."

"I told you I was going to have a lot of work done to the place this spring."

"What about robin-egg's blue?"

"No."

"Cantaloupe?"

"Eunice, I'm not going to allow you to paint the lab. Contractors will be handling the entire remodeling."

"If they can't spackle properly, how do you expect them to paint?"

Mitch chuckled and sadly shook his head. Eunice definitely needed a hobby. Last year at Christmas he had come to the conclusion that maybe she was a frustrated reincarnation of van Gogh and had bought her canvases and oil paints. She ended up painting an entire canvas red, had it professionally framed, and titled it "Imagination." When he had questioned her as to what it was supposed to be, she had said to use his imagination and imagine she could paint. Van Gogh she wasn't, but he had hung it in the living room anyway. Guests had stood in front of that painting swearing they could see images of everything from heaven's gate to cats sitting on a fence. It had become the family joke to test visitors.

"Go scrape the algae off the dining-room walls, Eunice, and stop worrying about the lab. The house has enough rooms to keep you busy until next fall."

Eunice muttered something about serving algae for dinner to unappreciative employers and left.

Mitch went back to grinning at the ceiling. Life was about to take a sharp corner marked COMPLI-CATIONS. He wondered if Hillary knew the difference between the colors Magnolia Blossom and Ever-So-Sweet. He wondered what she would do if he declared his love and proposed.

Last night had been a revelation. What they had shared wasn't just great sex, it had been deeper and gone straight to his heart. When Hillary had asked which character in Oz he would be, he hadn't told the truth. He wasn't the cute little mayor, he was the Tin Man. He had come to Oz and found his heart.

Seven

"I'm sorry, but I can't see anything," Hillary said, smiling apologetically at Eunice and Mitch. The picture on the wall was a beautiful shade of red, but that was just it. All it was was red. Not a speck of anything else could be seen. Normal people didn't go around beautifully framing a painting of nothing. "Maybe I'm blocking the light." She moved to one end of the room and studied it from that angle.

"Are you sure?" Eunice questioned.

Hillary bit her lip. She was about to make an enemy out of Mitch's housekeeper. "Positive."

Eunice and Callie chuckled. Mitch put an arm around Hillary's waist and gave her a quick hug.

A light, musical voice asked, "What's going on in here?"

Hillary turned to the doorway and saw a young woman standing there.

"Hillary," Mitch said, "I would like you to meet my sister, Ronnie."

She stared at the woman and then back at Mitch. He was serious. This was the same woman who came strolling through the backyard looking like a ten-dollar hooker the other day? Ronnie looked young and fragile in a huge purple sweatshirt, tight pink jeans, and bare feet. Her long brown hair was pulled back into a ponytail, and there wasn't a trace of makeup on her face. Veronica Ferguson could have been a model. She was gorgeous.

Hillary held out her hand and was surprised by the strength of Ronnie's grip. "Hello. Mitch has told me so much about you."

"I wish I could say the same about you." Ronnie raised a delicately arched brow at her brother.

"Ronnie, I would like to introduce you to Hillary Walker," Mitch said.

"Aunt Ronnie," Callie cried out, "Miss Walker didn't see anything in the picture."

"You didn't?" She hadn't missed the fact Mitch's arm was around Hillary, or that she was the same woman her big brother had been kissing in the yard the other day. Mitch had finally joined the living. "You have to forgive my brother's weird sense of humor. It comes from working with stinky old plastic all day."

Hillary glanced around the room looking for a clue as to what was going on. "Now you've totally confused me."

"You didn't know he worked with plastics?" Ronnie asked. That was unusual; Mitch tended to talk a person's ear off about recycling, the environment, and global warming.

"I know about his job." She waved a hand in the direction of the picture. "What's with the painting?"

Eunice chuckled. "Don't worry, honey, you passed the test with flying colors."

"What test?"

"It wasn't a test, Hillary," Mitch said. "It's more like a family joke."

Hillary stepped away from him. Being the brunt of some joke wasn't her idea of fun. She glared up at him and demanded, "What is it a painting of?"

"That's just it. It's a painting of nothing," Mitch explained. He smiled, confident that he had just cleared up the matter.

Hillary looked back at the painting. She had been right when she had said there wasn't anything there. So why had they laughed, and why did Callie seem so amazed? "What was I supposed to see?"

"You saw what you were supposed to see. Nothing."

Bewildered, she asked, "So what is the joke?"

Ronnie seemed to take pity on her. "Most people who see the painting swear they see all kinds of things in it. We all spend hours after they leave trying to detect what they saw."

That matter settled, Eunice headed for the kitchen. "Dinner's ready when you are."

Ronnie picked up a giggling Callie and threw her over her shoulder. She wrapped her other arm around Ethan, and headed for the dining room. Mitch anxiously shifted his weight from foot to foot. Maybe he shouldn't have quizzed Hillary on the painting. "I was just checking to see if insanity ran in your family."

Hillary glanced at his little-boy look, chuckled, and followed the laughing group out of the room. "It isn't *my* family hanging paintings of nothing in their home."

Mitch frowned as he watched her walk away. She was right. What kind of family would she be marrying into? His family had to accept only Hillary, while she had to adjust to him, two rambunctious children, his sister who thought she was indestructible, and Eunice the human paintbrush. No wonder he had been hesitant all week to declare his love and ask her to marry him. He wasn't sure if she would accept. He wasn't sure if he would accept such a proposal from Hillary if the situation had been reversed.

He entered the freshly painted Serenity-Green dining room and frowned. Hillary had been placed at the opposite end of the table from him, between Callie and Ethan. She was laughing out loud at a knock-knock joke Ethan had just told. The one thing he wanted was happening. Hillary and his kids were getting along. So why did he feel like swapping seats with Ethan? *Great! Now I'm jealous of my own kids.*

Hillary glanced up as Mitch plopped down in his chair and glared down the table at her. *Great! Question how many squirrels were in his family tree, and the man pouts.*

"So, Hillary, how did you meet my brother?"

Hillary glanced from Mitch to Callie. She couldn't tell Ronnie the truth, so over the delicious ham dinner she related the story of how she bumped into Mitch at the high school football game.

"You shouldn't encourage Eunice like that." Mitch took off his jacket and threw it over the back of a chair in Hillary's living room.

Hillary hung up her coat and turned on a second light. Dinner at Mitch's had been a revelation. She not only had a pleasant time, she had thoroughly enjoyed herself. "I wasn't encouraging her. I only gave my *asked-for* opinion."

He pulled her into his arms and lightly teased her mouth with a quick kiss. "Your opinion is going to cost me."

She smiled and tried to recapture his mouth for a more rewarding kiss. "Tell her no. It's your house."

Mitch's hands stroked her back. The fluffy sweater felt sensual under his fingertips. He had been dying all night to caress its softness. Hillary looked like an angel dressed in cream-colored satin pants and the sweater. Auburn curls that had escaped her French braid glowed in the light, giving the impression of a halo. His lips brushed her jaw. It had been less than twenty-four hours since he had made love to his angel, and he wanted her again.

Every night this week he'd tried balancing his obligation to his children and his desire for Hillary. It had been a hell of a balancing act. While he sat through dinners catching up on his children's day and helping with their homework, he wished he were with Hillary. As he lay in Hillary's big, soft bed holding her warm, satisfied body close to his, he worried that one of the kids would wake up, and he wouldn't be there.

Tonight he solved half the problem by having Hillary come to dinner. Only now he had another problem. "No can do. Once Eunice sets her mind on something, she won't rest until it's done." Detecting faint traces of Hillary's perfume behind her ear, he nuzzled the sensitive spot.

Hillary arched her neck to give him better access. "She's the one who dragged me into the kitchen."

"Did you have to suggest painting the cabinets white?"

Shivers of excitement ran through her as his teeth lightly scraped the beating pulse in her neck. "They're too dark and dreary-looking."

"But they're solid oak!"

Her fingers gently stroked his cheek. "They'll still be solid oak after you paint them."

How could he argue with the truth? With devilish delight he picked her up, carried her to the couch, and sat her on his lap. She could have suggested ripping out all the cabinets and replacing them with cardboard boxes, and he would have agreed. By the time his kids had had their baths and gotten ready for bed, Eunice and Hillary had a totally remodeled kitchen mapped out, with new flooring, countertops, and a custom-built island. Having two females design a new kitchen was twice as dangerous, and twice as costly. What one didn't think of, the other one did. Eunice had found a soul mate from painters' heaven. As soon as Hillary muttered the magical *P*-word, a lifelong bond had formed. Eunice's acceptance of Hillary into the household was guaranteed. "You and Eunice seemed to hit it off tonight."

"I'm surprised that no one in your family is overweight. That woman can cook, and what she did tonight with those potatoes was sinful." Hillary patted her flat stomach. "I barely had room for dessert."

Mitch wasn't about to tell her that all the special attention that had gone into the meal was because of her. Eunice had pulled out all the stops because Hillary was the first woman he had brought home for dinner since Catherine died. "What did you think of Ronnie?"

Ronnie had been the center of attention as she related one hysterical story after another during dinner. Her days on the force could inspire a sitcom. Of course, Hillary realized Ronnie was lightening them up for the children. When Ronnie had left for work, soon after dessert, she didn't look as if she were heading for a night of fun and games. Hillary sympathized with Mitch's concerns for his sister. "She's just like you."

Mitch was surprised by her observation. "In what way?"

Hillary snuggled deeper into his lap and wrapped her arms around his neck. His earthy after-shave teased her senses. It was the same scent he left behind on her pillow. Each night as she listened to the faint sound of his car leaving in the wee hours, she breathed in his scent and dreamed. "You're both cleaning up the world. You by using your brains and knowledge to lessen its garbage; Ronnie by using her courage to clean the human garbage from off our streets." Both were doing honorable and courageous things with their lives. So far her only claim to fame was making the world a better place for lispers and mumblers.

"I never thought of it that way," he said, slipping a hand under her sweater to gently rub her back. The faint stirring of her breath feathered his throat, and exquisite fingers played with the hair on the back of his neck. "Before I forget, Eunice wants me to invite you for Thanksgiving dinner, Thursday."

She opened her mouth and gently bit the side of his throat. "What do *you* want?"

Mitch realized his mistake. That had been a lousy way to invite someone to an important dinner. Thanksgiving was a time for family get-togethers. He wanted Hillary there. She was fast becoming a very important part of his family, and if he had his way, her value was about to go up. He pushed her back on the couch, carefully covering her body with his, then ravished her throat while making loud grunting noises. "I want *you* for Thanksgiving dinner."

Hillary laughed and wiggled under his weight. "Gobble, gobble," she managed to say just before the feel of his arousal against her thigh caused an "Ah" to escape her throat. The heated look in his eyes told her he wanted her. He wanted her here and now. They weren't going to make it to the downy softness of her bed tonight.

When she raised a finger and gently outlined the shape of his mouth, he captured her hand. His lips were hot and open as he pressed it to the center of her palm. With a flick of his tongue he lightly teased the sensitive skin, causing her nipples to bud and an aching emptiness to swell inside her. Only Mitch had the power to make her yearn so fiercely with just a look and the merest touch. "Oh, M-M-Mit-Mitch."

Her stuttering was his undoing. As the last ounce of control fled his body, he took her mouth in a heated kiss and stroked the passion till it consumed them both.

Mitch closed his eyes and groaned. It was worse than what he'd expected. He had spent two weeks worrying himself sick over how Hillary, Eunice, and Ronnie would get along, only for it to come to this: Total chaos. The three women in his life seemed to be on the same wavelength, driving Mitch over the edge by wreaking as much havoc as possible. Whatever happened to those nice peaceful Thanksgivings he remembered from his youth? The kind where Grandma wore a flowery apron and basted the turkey every half hour. The table would be set with the "good" china, and Norman Rockwell could have set up an easel in the corner of the room to preserve the occasion. Anyone crazy enough to enter willingly the free-for-all in his house deserved to have all sharp instruments placed out of his reach.

"Dad, have you seen a boat?" Callie asked.

Mitch looked down at his daughter and wondered if the madness that infected the three adult women was contagious. "Not since our summer vacation to the shore, why?"

"Ronnie asked me to look for one."

"Are you sure she said 'boat'?" It wasn't like his sister to send the kids on a wild-goose chase. He moved a box of baking pans and cookie cutters off a dining-room chair and set it on the floor.

Callie started to dig through another cardboard box. "Yep, she said 'boat.' A gravy boat."

Mitch glanced around the dining room and shook his head. He had no idea where to start looking for it. Boxes were piled on every available surface. He had to be as insane as everyone else in the house. He was the one who had given permission for Eunice to go ahead and start on the kitchen, mistakenly thinking she would wait until after Thanksgiving to begin the project. "Callie, it's not a real boat," he said, helping her look through the box.

"It's not?" Disappointment sounded in her voice.

"A gravy boat is a long bowl that holds the gravy. It can pour out of one end." He opened another box.

"Oh, good, you uncovered the table." Ronnie stood in the kitchen doorway and grinned. For the holiday she had dressed in her favorite outfit. A silk blouse decorated with hundreds of Donald Ducks hung to her thighs. Black stirrup pants and huge hairy-monster-feet slippers completed the outfit. She looked like a rebellious college student instead of a thirty-one-year-old cop.

Mitch glared at the slippers he had bought as a gag gift for her birthday last month. Why Hillary had not gone running from his home was a mystery to him. "Couldn't you have tried to dress nicer?" Last weekend Hillary had seen them on their best behavior; tonight was going to be rock bottom.

Ronnie wiggled her feet. Mitch had been acting grumpy all week, especially since Eunice called in a contractor. Men in love sure did some strange things, but remodeling a kitchen was new to her. Wouldn't it have been cheaper for Mitch to buy Hillary an expensive piece of jewelry? "Don't worry, Hillary loves them. She wanted to know where I got them. I told her I didn't know, since you bought them for me."

He closed his eyes and groaned. The small pounding headache that had started this morning had developed into a slew of jackhammers. "Where is Hillary?" He had lost sight of her after Eunice pushed him out of the demolished kitchen and into the dining room.

"Last time I saw her, she was peeling potatoes." Ronnie reached into a box and held up a garlic press. "What's this?"

He couldn't take much more. He'd invited to dinner the woman he planned on proposing to tonight, and his family had her peeling potatoes in a gutted-out kitchen.

He hurried into that room, and his heart stopped at the sight that greeted him. Hillary was standing on a stepladder using a steam machine to peel wallpaper off a wall. He hadn't thought the situation could get any worse, but Hillary had proven him wrong. "What are you doing?"

Hillary looked over her shoulder and grinned.

"Look, Mitch, I was right." She proudly waved her hand toward the wall. "Eunice said there were only three layers of wallpaper. I said there had to be at least four."

Eunice closed the oven door and grumbled, "Now I owe her one of my famous cherry cheesecakes."

Mitch's gaze never left Hillary. She looked utterly ridiculous standing barefoot on the third step of a ladder wearing a silk dress, pearls, and his barbecue apron with LIGHT MY FIRE printed across it. Her face was flushed, and her hair was giving new meaning to the word "frizz." She looked adorable. "Did you have to start peeling it now?"

"We still have another hour before dinner, right, Eunice?"

"Yes. It's going to take Ronnie that long to find all the dishes."

Mitch sighed. He had told Hillary dinner was at five. It was almost six now, and dinner was still in a holding pattern. How dinner was being cooked was a miracle in itself. The stove and refrigerator were pulled a couple of feet away from the walls. Empty cabinets with the doors hanging open were sanded and primed. Drawers stood against a wall, leaving gaping holes in the cabinetry. Half the countertops were missing, and most of the linoleum had been ripped from the floor. Mitch had considered it a small victory when he threatened bodily harm to the plumber if the water was shut off today and had won.

The table and chairs from the breakfast nook had been moved to the living room, which was currently being used to hold boxes of every linoleum and wallpaper sample known to man. The toaster was on the mantel, and the microwave oven was sitting on top of the television. Eunice had given new meaning to the term "TV dinners."

Mitch was still upset that Ronnie and Eunice both vetoed his idea of going out to eat at a nice restaurant. He had even volunteered to make the reservations himself. Their argument had been, if they ate Thanksgiving dinner in a restaurant, there wouldn't be any leftovers. By the look of his house, even if there were leftovers, no one would be able to find them.

He walked over to Hillary and unplugged the steam machine she was using. Then he reached up, placed his hands on her waist, and lowered her to the floor. His voice was low and seductive as he whispered, "If something is going to make you flushed and sweaty, it surely isn't going to be some steam machine."

Hillary gazed into his eyes and blushed a deep red. His meaning was perfectly clear. She edged away from him and placed the machine back where she'd found it. Her fingers trembled slightly as she fidgeted with the neckline of her dress and fanned herself. "Boy, can that machine throw out some heat."

Eunice glanced over at the couple and smiled knowingly.

Mitch started to chuckle as Hillary's face turned a shade redder. He reached for her hand and pulled her closer. "Come on, let's go for a walk. That should cool you down." He heard her mutter something about cold showers as he pulled her from the room.

Five minutes later Hillary found herself bundled in her coat, hiding behind the garage like a naughty teenager. She laughed and said, "I thought we were going for a walk?"

Mitch pressed her against the side of the building and blocked the blowing wind with his body. "I wouldn't be able to do this if we walked." He covered her mouth with his.

Moaning with pleasure, Hillary slid her arms around his neck. When she had arrived at his house for dinner, he had looked all squeaky-clean and scrumptious, his neatly combed hair still damp from the shower. She had wanted to run her fingers through it and mess it up, and now she did just that.

"Dinner's ready, Dad."

Mitch and Hillary jumped apart at the sound of Callie's voice. They both turned and stared at the grinning little girl, then Hillary buried her face in Mitch's jacket. What could she say to a child who'd caught her kissing her father?

Mitch's expression was a picture of guilt. He had been caught red-handed kissing Hillary behind the garage by his seven-year-old daughter. How should a father go about explaining this one? And shouldn't Callie be shocked instead of standing there grinning, looking quite pleased with herself? "Go ahead in, honey. We'll be right there."

"Okay, but Eunice says to hurry up, or we're starting without you." Callie turned and skipped around the side of the building.

Cupping Hillary's chin, Mitch forced her to look at him. "Are you all right?"

"Oh, Mitch, I'm sorry."

Amused, he asked, "For what? Kissing me?"

"No." She broke eye contact and stared at the white wall of the garage. "For being caught."

Mitch chuckled and pulled her into his arms. "Don't worry about it. Callie sees people kiss all the time."

Hillary looked up at Mitch, frowning. "She does?" Eunice didn't seem like the type to have a line of male friends banging on her door, and if Ronnie had a boyfriend, wouldn't he have been invited to dinner too?

He kept his arm around her as he led her back to the house. "Sure. You can't turn on television nowadays without seeing someone kissing." He didn't want Hillary to feel uncomfortable around his family, so he lightened the situation. He'd deal with Callie later, but for now he wanted to get through dinner so he could take Hillary home and pop the magic question.

The hallway was dim and shadowy late that night when Callie made her way to her brother's room. She pushed open his door and stepped inside. "Ethan?"

"Yeah?"

"Are you asleep?"

"No, what's the matter?"

Callie climbed up on his bed and tucked her pink flannel nightgown under her feet. "Do you want a baby brother?" She wasn't sure herself, but if Ethan said he did, she would take one.

Ethan sat up in a hurry. "What are you talking about?"

"I saw Daddy kissing Miss Walker behind the garage tonight."

"So?"

"My friend Ryan says his mommy and daddy kiss all the time, and he just got a new baby brother."

"That's because he has a mommy and a daddy. Miss Walker can't have a baby unless she marries Dad."

"Do you think they'll get married?"

"Sure they will." Ethan smiled. "They're kissing, aren't they?"

"But what about the baby brother?" Callie asked.

"Do you want Miss Walker to become our mother?"

"Yes."

"Since you and I like Miss Walker, and Dad seems to like her, then I guess we'll have to take the baby brother too." With that important issue solved, he said, "You were great tonight."

"I was?"

"Did you see the way she didn't yell at you when you spilled your milk all over the front of her dress?"

"But Dad started to."

"Only until Miss Walker stopped him. Not yelling at us is number ten on the list. We have half the list checked off now, thanks to you."

Callie got off the bed and headed for the door while Ethan scooted back under the covers. "Ethan?"

"Hmmm . . ."

"I didn't mean to spill my milk all over her," she

said in a weak and teary voice, then ran from the room. Ethan groaned. Girls were such sissies.

Mitch eyed the ruined green silk dress lying across the back of the chair. "I'll buy you a new one."

Hillary tied the sash on her robe and chuckled. "Don't be ridiculous. I'm sure the dry cleaners can clean it." She wasn't sure they could. She had never had eight ounces of milk spilled down on her before, but Mitch seemed obsessed with the stain.

Tonight everything seemed to grate on his nerves. She had never seen him so edgy and jumpy. She watched his reflection in the mirror as she took off her earrings and placed them in a crystal dish sitting on top of the bureau. Mitch was starting to wear down the carpet with his pacing. "Is everything going okay with the job?"

He jammed his hands into his pants pocket. The small jeweler's box felt tiny and insignificant in the palm of his hand, but it was the symbol of his hopes and dreams. "The job's fine," he answered, walking over to the window to stare out into her dark backyard.

She took off her necklace and dropped it into the crystal dish. Something was bothering Mitch, and she didn't know what. Over the past several nights their lovemaking had grown quite intense, and afterward he'd always seemed about to say something earthshattering, but for some reason he never did. Whatever it was, she wasn't sure she wanted to hear it. Things between them were going great. She didn't want them to change.

He jiggled the small black velvet box and continued to gaze into the night. "Sorry about dinner being so late."

"It was well worth the wait. Eunice is a dream." She pulled the ribbon from her hair and started to unravel the French braid. Performing her nightly routine in front of Mitch came as naturally as breathing. "You have to expect those types of delays when you're remodeling."

Mitch glanced over his shoulder at her. "Do you like what's being done to the kitchen?"

"You're going to have the most fantastic kitchen in Oz when it's done."

He turned completely around and studied her face. "You aren't just being nice, are you? You really didn't mind eating Thanksgiving dinner off unmatching plates or wearing my daughter's milk?"

"It could have been worse," Hillary said.

"How?"

"The food could have been lousy, and the milk could have been grape juice. I had a wonderful time tonight, and your family is terrific." She locked gazes with him in the mirror. "Now why don't you tell me what's really troubling you?"

He slowly walked across the room, stood behind her, and dropped a kiss on the tender skin on the nape of her neck. She didn't like the loving expression on his face. He didn't look like a man ready to break off a relationship. Instead he looked like a man set on making a commitment. Mitch was about to change the rules of the game, and she didn't know how to stop him.

His strong arms encircled her from the rear, and one of his hands pressed something against her abdomen that she couldn't see in the mirror.

With a sense of curiosity and dread she glanced down. Cupped in his large hand was a black jeweler's box. As she watched, transfixed, he flipped it open. There, nestled against black velvet, was the most gorgeous ring she had ever seen. The square-cut emerald glistened with a life of its own.

She raised her panic-stricken gaze back to the mirror.

Mitch grinned at her and forgot the loving proposal he had been practicing for days. "Put me out of my misery, Hillary, and marry me."

Eight

Hillary's gaze slid back to the ring. He wanted to marry her! Lord, now what was she supposed to do? Marriage, the ultimate commitment, was the fantasy of her youth. Mister Tall, Dark, and Handsome had popped the fifty-million-dollar question. She should be ecstatic, jumping for joy, and picking out wedding invitations. So why wasn't she? Because everything was happening too fast.

She had met Mitch only two weeks ago. Could she really be in love with him, or was she in love with the idea of being in love? How did a woman know she was in love? Did it hit her instantaneously, like a blinding flash that came from meeting someone's glance across a crowded room? Or did it grow slowly over time? Was it love she felt whenever Mitch walked into the same room, or was it merely the knowledge that they had great sex?

Hillary glanced back up at Mitch's reflection. He

was waiting for an answer she didn't have. Stalling for time, she said, "It's an emerald."

Mitch frowned. That wasn't the reply he had been hoping for. "I can always exchange it for a diamond." He really didn't care what gem it was, or even if it was a hunk of coal. He had picked out the emerald only because the Emerald City Jewelers specialized in emeralds, and he had thought it was romantic, considering they lived in Oz.

"Lord, no!" Hillary started to reach for the ring, then quickly dropped her hand as if the box would burn her. She moved out of his embrace and nervously glanced around the room. "I mean, the ring is gorgeous the way it is." She looked back at Mitch and muttered, "Being green and all."

"Emeralds usually are." Mitch snapped the box closed. "The answer's no, isn't it?"

Hillary chewed on her lower lip. "No."

"No? Is that the answer, or no the answer's not no?"

"No, the answer's not no." She didn't want to say no and lose Mitch. She knew what they had was special, but she wasn't sure how special. A yes would commit her to a lifetime of uncertainty. She wasn't going to walk into a marriage with the idea that they could work everything out later.

"Then the answer is yes?"

"No." She closed her eyes as Mitch groaned in frustration. "What I mean is, I don't know."

Incredulous, Mitch asked, "You don't know if you want to marry me?" He ran his fingers through his hair, noticing the tears pooling in her eyes.

"I need time." She silently pleaded with him for

understanding. "I can't make that kind of decision on a moment's notice."

Sighing in defeat, he walked over to the window and pressed his hand against the cool glass. He wasn't going to get his answer tonight, the night he'd thought his dreams would come true. But hard work and persistence were part of his nature. Once he made up his mind as to what he wanted, he used everything at his disposal to get it. And he wanted Hillary for his wife.

Hillary blinked back tears as she studied the carpet under her feet. She had insulted Mitch by not accepting his proposal. Could his ego stand the blow and grant her the time she desperately needed? "I'm sorry, Mitch."

He turned around and sadly shook his head, then walked over to her and gently cupped her chin. "You have nothing to be sorry for," he said, gazing into her moist eyes. "Take all the time you need, love, as long as you come up with the right answer."

His thumb tenderly brushed away a tear slowly making its way down her cheek. "I realize this has all happened kind of fast. We've barely known each other two weeks." His lips captured another teardrop. "But it's all the time I need to be sure I want to spend the rest of my life with you, Hillary."

Envious of his certainty, she asked, "How?"

"I didn't plan on it, and surely my life would have been a hell of a lot more uncomplicated if it hadn't happened. But it did. I fell in love with my daughter's speech teacher." He kissed her mouth, which had formed an *O* of surprise. "I love you, Hillary Walker."

I love you. With just those three simple words happiness filled her heart. Mitch seemed so positive of his feelings, she had to find out when he fell in love with her. "When did it happen?"

He genuinely smiled for the first time since proposing. "I knew I loved you the moment I opened the morning newspaper and saw your picture staring up at me. I wanted to kill the photographer and the congressman." He chuckled at her astonished look. "I wanted to purchase every newspaper in the state."

"To protect me?"

"No." He glanced down the front of her robe. "Your dress was hiked up, and I didn't want anyone else enjoying the view."

Hillary frowned. Seeing her picture in the morning paper was definitely not the moment when love bloomed in *her* soul.

Mitch didn't like the frown. He never should have mentioned the photo. He sat on the edge of the bed and drew her down next to him, holding her hand. "For days I practiced the speech I wanted to say tonight. I had the whole thing planned. We were going to have a perfect Thanksgiving dinner at my house. You were going to see what a wonderful family I have. When we got back to your house tonight, I was going to make slow, sweet love to you till dawn. As the sun rose in the sky and the new day began, I was going to tell you how much I loved you. You would echo the sentiments, and then I would ask you to marry me."

This was the perfect time for Hillary to declare her love, but she remained silent.

Mitch sighed and continued telling his daydream. "You say yes, and over breakfast in bed we discuss my children, Eunice, Ronnie, what to do with your house, what kind of dental floss you use. You know, all the important aspects of married life."

Hillary relived his daydream in her mind. It was a wonderful fantasy, but that was all it was—a fantasy. Her answer was going to be the same. Squeezing his hand, she said softly, "I need time, Mitch."

"I understand. It's a big responsibility taking on a husband and two kids. Not to mention Eunice, Ronnie, and a house without a kitchen." He released her hand and stood up. "I'm going to head home now."

"Why?"

He glanced from her to the big, empty bed behind her. He could lose himself in the heated softness of her body, but it wouldn't make his dream happen. "You need time, and I'm determined enough to give it to you." He bent and placed a light kiss on her mouth.

Hillary watched as he started to walk away. "Mitch?" He turned around. Her voice was gentle when she said, "Your family is wonderful."

He flinched, then murmured, "Thanks."

Hillary worried that he'd jumped to the wrong conclusion. She hadn't wanted him to think that her hesitation over marrying him had anything to do with his children. Ethan and Callie were great kids. He had done an excellent job of raising them. But now that he knew they were not the cause, he might believe *he* was.

He was halfway through the doorway when she

called out to him again. "Mitch, you forgot the ring." The small black box still sat on top of her bureau.

"No, I didn't. When you make a decision, either wear it or return it."

Hillary stared at the empty doorway long after she heard the front door close and his van drive away. Finally she got up, turned off all the lights, and crawled into bed.

Since when had it become too large for one person? Since a certain ecology-minded, gorgeous male had entered her life, that's when. Though she couldn't make out the jeweler's box in the darkness, it seemed to mock her torment.

All she had to do was open it, slip on the ring, and her bed would never be lonely again.

The following evening Hillary glared at the news anchorman on the television and silently demanded what right he had to be so cheerful. He had just reported a double murder, a three-car pileup, and a high-pressure system that looked as though it was going to dump six inches of snow on them by Sunday. The whole day had started off lousy and had gotten worse as it progressed.

This morning, after spending a sleepless night, she had scrubbed the house from top to bottom and managed to put away three chocolate-covered doughnuts. By noon she had driven thirty miles to a craft show she had been looking forward to attending. No cute animals jumped out and said "Buy me," but an apple pie had her name written all over it. Two very small pieces were left, and as soon as she picked up some more vanilla ice cream, they would be history.

Since the craft show was close to her parents' house, she had stopped in to visit and ended up staying for dinner. It didn't taste as good as last night's meal. Maybe it was the fact that the dishes consisted of Thanksgiving leftovers, or maybe it was the company. She loved her parents, but after thirty-one years she knew what they were going to say before they said it. No one spilled the milk, and all the plates matched. It had been a perfectly civilized and refined occasion. She had missed the laughter and unpredictability in the Fergusons' house. She had missed Mitch.

She glared from the chuckling newsanchor to the open jeweler's box now sitting on the coffee table. The emerald ring sparkled against the black velvet. She had hidden the box in four different spots before settling on taking it with her to the craft show. No one knew about the ring, but she couldn't chance someone breaking in and stealing it. The tiny box had been nestled securely in the bottom of her purse. If people stared at her for clutching her purse as if it contained the Hope Diamond, that was their problem. She had enough of her own.

The answer to Mitch's question still evaded her. She wasn't 100 percent sure. Hell, it was more like 75 percent yes and 25 percent don't know. The no's hadn't voiced themselves all day; it was the don't knows that caused her to hesitate. How was she going to be 100 percent sure?

Hillary jerked as someone knocked on her front door. Who could that be at this time of night? She

hurried across the room, thinking it had to be
Mitch. With one hand on the doorknob, she
asked, "Who is it?"

"Mitch."

Her fingers fumbled in their haste to take off the
chain and it took her twice as long to open the
door, but it was well worth the wait. Mitch stood
on her porch looking impatient and sexy. Her
voice was breathless as she whispered, "Hi."

Mitch walked into the house and closed the door
behind him. Before Hillary could utter another
word, he hauled her into his arms and kissed her.

The kiss was hard, long, and demanding. His
breath was coming in harsh gasps when he finally
lifted his head and muttered, "Lord, I missed you."

Her lips were swollen and pink from his kiss,
but they managed to smile beautifully anyway. He
had come. "Not half as much as I missed you."

Mitch locked the door and picked her up, his
steps sure and steady as he started down the hall
toward the bedroom.

"Mitch?"

"Hmmm?" His lips had found the rapidly beating pulse in her throat.

"I'm still not sure," she said, a slight frown
wrinkling her brow.

He raised his head and gazed at her troubled
face. "Don't worry, love, I'm sure enough for us
both." His feet continued their journey.

"You don't have to apologize, Mitch." Hillary
gazed at the phone in disbelief. Did the man really
believe she would be upset and not understand

why he wasn't coming tonight? "How high is her temperature?"

"Hundred and one."

"Have you given her Tylenol?" The thought of little Callie lying in bed burning up with a fever tore at her heart. She must have caught the nasty bug that was going around the school.

"Yes. She's due to take another tablet in about an hour."

Concerned, she asked, "Has she eaten anything?"

"Not much. I did manage to get half a cup of tea and three bites of toast in her though."

Hillary could hear the fatigue and worry in his voice. Mitch had obviously spent the entire day taking care of his daughter. "I'd better let you go so you can get back to her."

"Eunice is up there now trying to entertain her with a Barbie tea party."

Laughter escaped Hillary's throat at the vision of Eunice serving tea to a bunch of dolls. "You better watch out, or Eunice will have Barbie and her friends putting on smocks and repainting Barbie's Dream House."

Mitch chuckled. "You may have a point there. I'd better get back."

"Good-bye, Mitch."

"Hillary?"

"Yes?"

"I love you." There was a click on the line as he hung up.

Hillary stared at the silent receiver clutched in her hand. For the past week Mitch had said those words to her countless times, and they still brought her happiness. She hadn't been able to give Mitch his answer, but each new day with him in her life she was a little more certain. She didn't know what she would do if Mitch walked out of her life now.

She slowly replaced the receiver and glanced at the clock. It was only six o'clock. In the past Mitch had always come to her. Maybe it was time she went to him.

Mitch wondered about the commotion going on downstairs. He glanced from his daughter's flushed face to the book he held. His voice was going hoarse from reading the story about some little girl and her pet pig, Wilbur. "How about if I go make us another cup of tea?"

Callie hugged her stuffed rabbit tighter. Peter had been around as long as she could remember and had gone through everything with her. His button eyes didn't match anymore, and his one remaining ear was stained from grape jelly, but she would never give him up. Nothing bad would ever happen to her as long as he was around. He was her most trusted friend. "I'm not thirsty, Daddy."

Mitch brushed back her bangs from her forehead. "I know, sweetheart, but I want you to try to drink something."

She was cold and shaky, and she felt sick to her stomach. Her eyes were watery as she whispered, "Okay, I'll try."

"That's my girl." Mitch kissed her warm cheek,

then stood up and walked to the door. "I'll be right back."

The sound of banging pots and voices could be heard from the top of the stairs. He hurried down the steps and headed for the kitchen. As he neared it, one voice in particular caught his attention. He stopped in his tracks as he entered the room. Hillary was standing at the newly installed island chopping celery.

She was wearing a Washington Redskins' sweatshirt and faded jeans. Piles of vegetables, boxes of crackers, and cartons of orange juice were spread out on the counter. Ethan was sitting on a stool munching on a raw carrot and busily telling her what he had done with his day. Eunice was folding the paper grocery bags and looking quite pleased with having her domain invaded by Hillary.

Mitch finally found his voice and asked, "What's going on here?" Three pairs of eyes turned toward him.

"I'm making my delicious chicken-vegetable soup," Hillary answered.

He lifted the lid off the huge pot on the stove and saw cut-up chicken covered with bubbling water inside. Hillary cared enough about Callie to come rushing over and start a marathon of cooking. Things were looking up. He walked over to Hillary and, not caring who was in the room, kissed her. "Thank you."

Then he glanced at his wide-eyed son and said, "Ethan, please keep your sister company for a few minutes."

Ethan hurried from the room, dashed up the

steps, and ran into Callie's bedroom. "Callie, guess what?"

The little girl opened her eyes. "What?"

"Miss Walker's downstairs making you a pot of soup."

That Miss Walker was here was okay, but the soup didn't appeal to her at all. She wished her tummy didn't hurt so bad.

Ethan sat down in a chair next to the bed. "I told her soup wasn't one of your favorite things to eat, and do you know what she said?"

"What?"

"That once you get better, she was going to bake you the most delicious chocolate cake you ever tasted."

"She did?"

"Do you know what that means?" Ethan looked questioningly at his sister. "It means we got an answer to number seven. Miss Walker can bake some neat stuff."

Callie smiled faintly, closed her eyes, and hugged Peter Rabbit. "That's nice," she said in a scratchy voice. Within an instant she was asleep.

Hillary stood in front of the toy-store window and watched the electric train weave its way through a miniature snow-covered village. Christmas was two weeks away, and she hadn't even started her shopping. She pulled the collar up on her jacket and studied the surrounding stores. The Yellow Brick Road Shopping Center was a beehive of activity. Shoppers hurried from store to store struggling under the weight of their packages, while Christmas carols filled the air. Huge red bows decorated the old-fashioned streetlights, and every store was decked out in Christmas finery. Someone had even tied a bow around the giant Tin Man statue made out of stainless steel. The town of Oz was getting ready for Santa's yearly flight.

She walked to the Munchkin Land apparel shop next door and smiled at one of the mannequins in the window. Callie would look adorable in that outfit. But what child wanted to get clothes for Christmas? Hillary walked back to the Cowardly Lion Toy Emporium and watched the train again. What nine-year-old boy wouldn't love a train?

She was looking at the rest of the toys displayed in the window, wondering what Callie might like, when other shoppers started to stop and stare into the sky. Amazed, Hillary watched as even shopkeepers came out and stared upward.

"Who's Hillary?" asked an older woman.

Hillary immediately glanced upward. A small silver-and-blue plane was pulling a banner. There, in huge red letters, were the words SURREN-DER HILLARY!

She couldn't control her laughter. Last night Mitch had said he was going to start pulling out the heavy artillery if she didn't give him the answer he wanted soon. Well, it looked as though the heavy artillery included an air force. What was next? Hiring an army of winged monkeys to carry her off?

The older woman and man next to her stared at each other and then at Hillary. "Are you Hillary?"

Six other shoppers stared at her.

Hillary looked back up at the plane still circling the heavens. "I'm afraid so."

Curious, the woman asked, "Are you at war?"

"No," she answered, smiling. "It's a marriage proposal."

With a serious expression on his face, the man asked, "Are you going to accept?"

Hillary's gaze followed the banner as it made another circle over Oz. "Yes, I believe I am." She wasn't amazed that she had finally answered Mitch's question; she was astounded by how right the answer had felt.

Mitch entered the dining room and noticed an extra place setting at the table. He looked over at his children and Ronnie, who were already seated. "Who's coming to dinner?"

Hillary walked out of the kitchen carrying a huge bowl of mashed potatoes. "I am." She set the bowl on the table. "Have any objections?"

"Not a one." He wrapped his arms around her and gave her a quick kiss. She looked gorgeous in a soft creamy-colored dress, with her hair left down, wild and free. Callie giggled at the kiss. "When did you get here?"

"While you were showering." She leaned in closer and whispered, "I would have joined you, but I didn't want to shock poor Eunice." Her fingers briefly stroked his jaw.

He groaned and tightened his hand on her hips. "I'll fire her in the morning."

"Good." She looked over at Eunice, who had just

entered the room carrying a platter piled with roast beef. "I wonder if she'd come work for me."

Mitch chuckled and pushed Hillary away. He didn't know why she'd shown up for dinner, but he was glad she had. He had been dying all day to know if she had seen his newest attempt at winning her heart. After helping Hillary in her chair and taking his own, he innocently asked, "So, Hillary, what did you do all day?"

"Shopped." She passed Ronnie the bowl of string beans.

"In town?"

She thanked Eunice for handing her the biscuits, then said, "At the Yellow Brick Road Shopping Center. I did almost all my Christmas shopping." She looked over at Ethan and Callie and gave them a meaningful look. "The toy store there had some wonderful gifts."

Ethan and Callie grinned at each other.

Frowning, Mitch held the platter of meat for Hillary. "Isn't that the place where you have to walk outside to get from store to store?"

Hillary kept her face straight as she selected a piece of beef. Mitch was so caught up in trying to find out if she had seen the skywriting that he was missing what was right under his nose. "Yes, it is." With her left hand she raised a glass of water to her lips.

He started to eat as Eunice complained about the size of the Christmas tree Mitch had brought home. Every year it was the same old fight. Eunice always wanted a huge fresh-cut pine tree that would stretch from floor to ceiling and from wall to wall. The old saying about the bigger, the better, held true with Eunice and her Christmas spirit. Every year Mitch purchased a small live tree with its roots still attached so he could plant it after Christmas. He couldn't see killing a tree just to throw some tinsel on it and place a few brightly wrapped presents under it.

Eunice had just gotten to the part about how she was going to have to repack half the ornaments because the tree was so small, it wouldn't hold them all, when Mitch started to choke.

Eunice stopped talking, and everyone stared at Mitch.

He finally swallowed what was in his throat and breathed. His finger pointed down the table at Hillary. "You . . . you . . . you . . ."

Hillary wiggled the third finger of her left hand. The emerald ring blazed under the light from the chandelier above. Hallelujah, he'd finally noticed. When Mitch continued to stare silently at her hand, she smiled and said the word he had been waiting for: "Yes."

Mitch's gaze went from the ring to her face. Did she say what he thought she had said? "Yes?"

She slowly nodded her head. "Yes." She still wasn't 100 percent sure, but she had gone over it so many times in her head that she was doubting she had doubts. When she had tried to visualize what her life would be without Mitch and his family, she couldn't. Her whole life was Mitch. It had to be love, there was no other word for it. When she had looked up into the sky and seen the banner, she knew this was the man she wanted to spend the rest of her life with.

His fork hit the plate with a clatter as he jumped

up and hurried to Hillary. He pulled her from her chair and swung her around in circles. "How? When?" He stopped swinging her and quickly kissed her. "Hell with it. Who cares?"

Ronnie and Eunice both looked highly entertained by the show the couple was putting on. "Would either of you care to enlighten the rest of us?" Ronnie asked.

Mitch put his arm around Hillary and announced, "Hillary has just consented to become by wife."

Ronnie and Eunice smiled at each other and in unison said, "Finally."

Ethan and Callie grinned, raised their arms high in the air, and smacked each other's hand while shouting, "Yeah!"

Mitch breathed a sigh of relief at his family's reaction and pulled Hillary back into his embrace for another kiss. "My feelings exactly."

Nine

Hillary giggled and moved to the edge of the mattress. "Stop that." Ever since she had said yes earlier that evening, Mitch had been impossible. They had celebrated the engagement during dinner by breaking out a bottle of wine. Ronnie had complained that she could have only a sip or two because she had to report to work soon, and Eunice griped that it should have been champagne. Ethan and Callie had an orange drink and were allowed seconds on dessert.

Mitch nuzzled the back of her neck with his lips. "Never."

She squirmed as his lips found her shoulder. The man had obviously recovered from their previous lovemaking. After the kids had calmed down and fallen asleep, Mitch had followed her to her house. They had barely made it inside before their passion erupted. Coats, clothes, and shoes were still scattered around her living room. Their love-making had never been as hot or explosive.

Mitch's fingers stroked the curve of her hip. "Do you really want me to stop?"

She rolled onto her back and smiled. "Not on your life."

Mitch raised himself on one elbow and grinned down at her. She looked so tempting with her wild hair spread out across the pillow and her lips puffy and red from his kisses. Gently caressing her cheek, he said, "Would you think I'm a chauvinist pig if I bang on my chest and shout, 'Mine, mine, mine' for all the world to hear?"

"It would be a cute gesture, a tad excessive, but cute."

Disbelieving, he asked, "You wouldn't mind?"

"Try it, and I'll throw you out of here." She reached up and tugged on the curls covering his chest. "If anyone's going to bang on you, it had better be me."

Mitch lay back down and pulled her on top of him. Heated flesh of legs and arms tangled together. The tightly wound hair at the juncture of her thighs brushed against his arousal. "We still haven't set the date." Now that he had her promise to marry him, he wanted a date. The sooner, the better. He wanted her in his bed for the rest of his life.

Hillary felt her nipples harden as his manhood nudged her thigh. "Now?" She flexed her hips. "You want to discuss wedding dates now?"

He cupped a breast and brought the straining nipple to his lips. "I can't think of a better time."

"Well, I can." She pressed herself against him,

trying to complete the union, but he moved away.

He wasn't taking any chances; he wanted a date set tonight. "Are you still against the kids' suggestion of a Christmas wedding?" he asked, teasing the other nipple.

She arched her back. "There's no way we can pull off an entire wedding in two weeks."

"Eunice and Ronnie said they'll help."

Her fingers gripped his thighs. "I was thinking maybe June."

"Too far away. I'll never make it." He bit his lip trying to hold on to his control.

"Easter?"

His fingers slid past the curls to slip inside her. "No."

Her hips slowly rocked against his hand. At a time like this how was she supposed to think about dates? "What do you have in mind?"

New Year's Day sounded great to him, but he didn't want to rush her. She apparently had some idea of what kind of wedding she wanted. "Valentine's Day."

"That's only two months away!" Mitch withdrew his hand. "Okay, okay. Valentine's Day it is."

He had his woman, and now he had a date. He clutched her hips and plunged into her heat.

She changed their rhythm to a frantic pace of her own. The man had played dirty pool to get his way. If she had to play the game, she wanted to at least be in charge.

Mitch felt his control shattering and wanted to hold back the waves of pleasure building in their intensity. Crying out her name, he tried to still her.

She heard the ecstasy and torment in his voice and fought his control. She wanted to take them both over the edge she was clinging to. The rhythm increased. Her thighs pressed against his hips, and her silken walls tightened around him.

He followed her blindly over the edge, chanting her name with every harsh breath he took.

Mitch brushed at the auburn curls clinging to his jaw. Hillary lay exhausted, across his chest, and their legs were still entwined. His breathing had finally returned to normal, and guilt was riding his soul. He never should have used sex to force an answer from her. "That was a rotten thing for me to do."

Hillary's eyes didn't open. "Yes, it was." If there was one thing she'd learned about Mitch over the weeks, it was that he was fair and loving. He must have wanted to set a date desperately.

"I won't hold you to Valentine's Day."

She rubbed her cheek against his chest. He made a wonderful pillow. "That's a shame." She liked the idea of getting married on the most romantic day of the year.

"It is?"

"Callie would look adorable dressed in red."

Mitch cupped her chin and made her look up at him. "You mean it? Valentine's Day is okay with you?"

"If there were only you and me to consider, I'd marry you tomorrow. But that isn't the case. Eunice and Ronnie have already started making lists, and Ethan and Callie would be very disappointed if they weren't in the wedding." With impish delight she added, "Besides, my father would kill you if you didn't give him the opportunity to walk me down an aisle."

He chuckled and brought her mouth within inches of his. "Have I told you how much I love you today?"

"About six times." She brushed her lips across his.

"Make it seven."

"But, Dad, we don't have all the questions answered yet," Callie said.

Confused, Mitch looked at his daughter. "What are you talking about? I thought you and Ethan were happy Hillary and I are getting married."

"Shut up, Callie," Ethan snapped.

Mitch's gaze immediately swung to his son. His two children were definitely up to something. "What's going on, Ethan?"

"Nothing."

"Ethan," Mitch said, his voice deep with authority.

Ethan's chin rose a notch. "I like Miss Walker, Dad, and I'm glad you're getting married."

Mitch wasn't fooled for a moment. "What questions is Callie talking about?"

"I don't know."

"The list, Ethan," Callie said, ignoring his murderous glare. "You know, Ethan, the one you carry around with you all the time."

Mitch held out his hand. This morning when he had sat down with his kids to find out what concerns they might have about his upcoming marriage, everything had seemed wonderful. Ethan and Callie both liked Hillary and were looking forward to finally getting a mother. When he had told them the date had been set for Valentine's Day, Callie had voiced her first concern— the unanswered questions.

Glaring at his sister, Ethan dug the crumpled list from his back pocket and give it to his father.

Mitch opened the folded piece of paper. It was a list of ten things, titled "What Kids Look for in a Mother." Six of the items were already crossed off. His kids had been grading Hillary against some article in a kids' magazine. Mitch burst out laughing.

Ethan and Callie looked at their father and relaxed.

He couldn't believe it. He glanced back down at the list and continued to laugh. The proof was in his hand, and he still couldn't fathom it. They were judging Hillary by a list compiled from answers from one thousand kids aged eight to twelve nationwide, if the small print at the bottom of the article was to be believed.

Ethan asked, "You aren't mad?"

Mitch slowly shook his head. "No, Son, I'm not mad. I want you and your sister to like Hillary for who she is and not because of some list though."

"We do like Miss Walker," Callie said. "She even does stuff that's not on the list." She looked at her brother for support. None was forthcoming. "We're really happy you're getting us a mom, but how are we going to answer the rest of the questions?"

Mitch studied his children. Ethan had just turned four and Callie no more than a toddler when Catherine had died in an auto accident. Their memories of their mother were vague if not nonexistent. To them the list represented the ideal mother. Mitch wanted them to have their ideal mother. He knew the kids would fall in love with Hillary as they got to know her better, but Valentine's Day was only two months away. If passing this test would get the marriage off on steadier ground, he was all for it. "How about if I help you find out the rest?"

Ethan's eyes widened. "You mean it?"

"Sure, I bet we can finish off this list by Christmas."

"Mitch, I think we might have a problem." Hillary tugged at his arm and pulled him out of the crowded living room.

He wickedly smiled as he backed her up against the hallway wall and kissed the enticing pout of her lower lip. "Yeah, too many people. Whose idea was this anyway?"

"Yours." Her arms circled his waist. "You're the one who wanted to meet my parents and brother."

"I was hoping for something a little more relaxed and orderly." The nice informal dinner had turned into "Wedding Arrangements 101." Eunice, Ronnie, Hillary's parents, and her brother, Matt, were boisterously discussing every aspect of the wedding. Lists on who was to handle what detail littered the coffee table. By the amount of noise and confusion, and by the alarming pages of lists, someone would think a Vanderbilt was getting married. "What's the problem? Does Ronnie want to do an I.D. search on all the guests?" He could kid about her job now that "the Ripper" had been caught and was safely behind bars.

"Worse. Eunice wants to redo the master bedroom for our wedding present."

Mitch groaned and pressed his forehead against the wall. "Do we have a choice?"

"Not if you want to keep eating. I don't know about you, but most of the time I nuke my dinners."

He pulled her closer to him and kissed her ear. "I'll keep you anyway."

Hillary savored the feel of his lips. The past week had been fantastic. No woman could wish for a better fiancé. Mitch was not only a phenomenal lover, but he was also equally attentive out of bed. Her feelings for him had grown stronger and more powerful since she'd put on his ring. The doubts were down to below one percent. Ninety-nine-point-forty-four percent positive, she thought her love for him was like the famous bar of soap—unsinkable.

Still, she couldn't bring herself to tell Mitch she loved him, not until she was 100 percent sure. That .56 percent of doubt haunted her. Hadn't everyone said the *Titanic* was unsinkable too? Her relationship with Mitch was sailing on smooth seas, with not an iceberg in sight. But Hillary couldn't stop looking out for icebergs.

"Hillary?"

Mitch and Hillary jumped apart like guilty teenagers as her mother entered the hall. "Yes, Mom?"

"We need you to settle something." Mrs. Walker was in her late fifties, and except for having shorter hair, ten more pounds, and a few extra wrinkles, she bore a stunning resemblance to Hillary. Mitch had liked her on sight.

"You want red and white as your color theme, right?"

"Yes," Hillary answered.

"Eunice and I have been discussing it, and we decided you need another color. If you only have white and red, the whole effect would be"—she waved her hands in the air—"candy-canish."

"Candy-canish? Really, Mom, I don't think there's such a word."

"How can I put this delicately, Hillary?" She thought for a moment and stated, "If you don't add another color, the people in your wedding party are going to look like barber-shop poles."

Mitch cracked up laughing. Hillary glared at her future husband. He wasn't the one who had to come up with a coordinating color and make all the decisions at the drop of a hat. "What is it you wanted me to settle, Mom?"

"Eunice says you should use pink, the wedding being on Valentine's Day and all." She looked at Mitch, clearly hoping to gain his support. "The pink and red would clash, dear. Don't you think so, Mitch?"

Mitch didn't care if all the bridesmaids were naked. He only cared about Hillary saying "I do" and a preacher pronouncing them man and wife. Smiling dutifully at his future mother-in-law, he replied, "Whatever Hillary decides is fine by me."

Hillary snorted. "What color did you pick, Mom?"

"Black. Black is very big in weddings nowadays."

Hillary bit her lip. She had to agree with her mom about the pink, but black was equally out. She closed her eyes and thought.

"Well, honey, what will it be—black or pink?"

"Neither." She looked at her mother and smiled. "Silver. I want silver."

"Are you sure?" Mrs. Walker looked unconvinced. "I never saw bridesmaids wearing silver before."

Hillary walked into the living room with her mother right on her heels and headed for the platter of brownies and cookies Eunice had set out. "Then I guess I'm going to start a new trend." She picked up a brownie. She needed a sugar surge to keep up with Eunice and her mother. By the time Valentine's Day finally came, they were going to have to roll her down the aisle.

Hillary huddled deeper into her coat and pulled the thick collar up around her ears. She had picked a lousy day to forget her earmuffs and scarf. Recess duty had to be the low point in every teacher's week. For a half hour she had to stand outside, with the bitter wind freezing unmentionable parts of her body and 112 monsters trying to do one another bodily harm. She jerked as a rubber ball slammed into her back. At the next union meeting she was going to request combat pay for recess duty, double-time when there was a kickball game on.

"Sorry, Miss Walker."

Hillary forced a pleasant smile, picked up the ball, and handed it back to the eight-year-old hellion. "That's okay, Paulette. Next time try to be more careful, you don't want to hurt anyone."

Paulette smiled angelically and ran back to the game. Within an instant she was hurling the ball at a boy who was running from second base to third. Hillary shook her head and ignored the game. There were more menacing activities going on in the playground. Somewhere in the mass of brightly colored coats, hats, and mismatched mittens, future felons were lurking and developing their skills.

There was only one thing worse than pulling recess duty two days before Christmas break, and that was having it the day before. She pitied the poor teacher who had pulled it tomorrow. The children were already literally bouncing off the walls to the point of being uncontrollable.

Hillary spotted Callie and Ethan talking to a group of other students. Callie's hat was sticking out of her coat pocket. She remembered how sick Callie had been a few weeks back and walked over to the group. No one noticed her approach.

"He is too!" Callie cried out. "Tell him, Ethan."

Ethan proudly lifted his chin and grinned. "She's telling the truth, Nathan. Our dad's getting us a mom for Christmas."

"How's he doing that?" Nathan asked. Having a mom wrapped up and sitting under the tree Christmas morning sounded dumb to him.

"He's marrying her, stupid," Ethan snapped. Second graders were so dumb.

Callie looked at her classmates and said, "Guess who my mommy will be?"

The kids stared at one another, bewildered. Their mommies had always been there. Their daddies didn't have to get them one for Christmas.

Callie glanced up and spotted Hillary standing there. "Miss Walker!" Callie moved closer to her and took her hand. "Tell them, Miss Walker."

"Tell them what?" She knew what Callie wanted her to tell them, but she didn't want to let them know she had been listening.

"That my dad's marrying you."

Hillary smiled at the group of students. "Callie's right, guys. I'll be marrying her father."

Eyes widened and mouths fell open. Not many of the kids could think of anything worse than having a teacher for a mother.

Hillary laughed at their expressions. Second graders weren't very good at hiding their true feelings. "The wedding will be held on Valentine's Day."

Nathan looked at Callie. "I thought you said she was going to be your Christmas present?"

Hillary sighed with relief as the recess bell sounded. "Everyone line up." She looked at Ethan and Callie. "When school's over, you two come to my room. I'll give you a ride home." She apparently had a couple of things to straighten out with her future stepchildren.

Hillary poured three glasses of milk, piled some cookies onto a plate, and set them in front of

Ethan and Callie, who were sitting in her kitchen gazing around with great interest. She had already called Eunice to tell her she had the kids and that she would be driving them home later.

After a few minutes of snacking and discussing her cow collection, Hillary decided to take the bull by its horns. "Callie, why did you tell Nathan that your daddy was getting you a mother for Christmas?" she asked.

Callie took a swallow of milk. "Because he is."

"I think you misunderstood, honey. Your father and I are getting married in February, over six weeks after Christmas. I won't be your mommy until then."

"I know that." Callie reached for another cookie. "But you're still my present."

Bewildered, she asked, "How am I your present?"

"I asked for a mommy, and you passed the test."

"You wanted a mommy for Christmas?" Hillary asked incredulously.

"So did Ethan. We've been asking for one for the last two years."

Hillary looked at Ethan. Maybe he would make more sense. "Ethan, what test did I pass?"

Ethan proudly pulled the list from his back pocket and handed it to her. "This one."

She carefully opened the much-handled slip of paper. Her mouth fell open in utter disbelief as she read the list. Ethan and Callie had been testing her all along. She read every requirement again and couldn't fathom how she had managed to pass this test. Item number one was, *Doesn't make you clean up your room.* Last Saturday she had taken them shopping so they could buy their father a Christmas present. Before they had walked out the door, Mitch had questioned them if their rooms were clean. When they had hesitated, she had said something about letting them clean up later.

Another requirement was that she like snakes and other icky animals. She broke out in hives just thinking about snakes and other slimy, crawly creatures. One day a student, Johnny, let a frog loose in her classroom. She had been so scared, she couldn't even scream. Ethan and Callie were going to be mighty disappointed with their new mother.

Unsure how to proceed, she asked, "Does your father know about this list?" Mitch was sure to figure out how to handle the situation—after all, they were his kids.

"Sure." Ethan beamed. "He was the one who helped us get some of the answers."

"He was?" She stared down at the crumpled list. *Mitch had helped them with this? Why would he do that?* She suddenly started to have doubts about becoming an instant mother. Kids were a lot harder to understand than she'd originally thought. "What does this have to do with me being your Christmas present?"

"Every year Dad makes us write out a 'Wish List' for Christmas," Callie said. "Last year, me and Ethan asked for a mommy and a bunch of other stuff." Disappointment filled her voice. "We got the other stuff, but no mom."

Hillary felt her heart lurch as she stared at the

little girl. How could you explain to a little girl that Santa didn't bring mommies?

"This year we did it differently," Ethan said.

"You did?"

"Yeah, we only asked for one thing this time," Callie said. "You!"

"Me?"

"Yeah," Ethan answered. "We decided to give up the toys and stupid clothes we always get so we can have you." He finished off his glass of milk, leaving behind a white mustache on his upper lip. "Me and Callie picked you out ourselves." His voice held the pride he felt.

Not wanting to be left out, Callie said, "Miss Thomas, the town librarian, was our second choice." She looked at Hillary's striken face, and quickly added, "But we thought you would be more fun."

Hillary couldn't believe it. They had planned the whole thing, from Callie's baby talk to asinine lists on how to judge a mother. And Mitch had gone along with it all. She should have seen it coming. Mitch had freely admitted on numerous occasions that his children were the most important thing in his life and that he would do anything for them. They had wanted a mom, and she was their first choice. Mitch was marrying her because of the children.

The *Titanic* had hit an iceberg and was sinking fast. She had been so blinded by her growing love for Mitch, she hadn't seen it coming. Whoever said love was blind was only half-right. It was also deaf and stupid.

"Thank you for thinking I'll make a great mom."

What else could she say at this point? "Let's get your coats on, and I'll run you home." The fingers holding the list started to tremble. Her whole life had just fallen apart. "Ethan, can I keep this?"

"Sure, I don't need it anymore."

Fifteen minutes later she parked the car in Mitch's driveway and stared at the garage. Mitch was in there working on some experiment combining cornstarch with polystyrene to make bio-degradable foam packages. "You kids go ahead and tell Eunice you're here. I want to talk to your father privately for a few minutes."

Ethan started for the house, but Callie hung back. "Miss Walker?"

"Yes, Callie?" She hoped whatever Callie wanted would be quick. The tears she had been holding back were ready to start flowing.

"Me and Ethan talked about it, and we won't mind getting a baby brother."

"What baby brother?" Oh Lord, wouldn't this nightmare ever end? What was she talking about now?

"The one you get from kissing." Callie turned and followed her brother into the house.

Hillary's gaze stayed on the back door long after the children had disappeared inside. She was going to miss them almost as much as she'd miss Mitch. She blinked back the flood of tears crowding her eyes, straightened her shoulders, and walked over to the lab.

Mitch glanced up as Hillary opened the door and walked in. "Hi, stranger." He hadn't seen her since leaving her bed sometime before dawn.

She twisted the emerald ring off her finger,

walked over to the work counter where Mitch was sitting, and very carefully laid it down. "It's been an experience."

He glanced from the ring to her pale, striken expression. "What's going on?"

Hillary took a deep breath. "The wedding's off." There, she had said it. The dream of her youth had crumbled.

Mitch stood up and reached for her. She stepped back. He slowly dropped his hands. Confused, he asked, "Why?"

"I won't marry a man who doesn't love me." Her voice broke on the word "love," but she managed to finish the sentence.

"What in the hell are you talking about?" Mitch roared. He had never heard of anything more absurd.

She took another step back. "You're only marrying me to please the kids. I won't be anyone's Christmas present," she replied, brushing away the tears sliding down her cheeks.

Mitch frowned. She was serious. She really thought he was marrying her only to please his children. He moved closer. "Oh, honey."

"Don't you 'honey' me! I've seen the list, Mitch. You were helping them!" She moved closer to the door, threw the crumpled list at him, and grabbed the doorknob. "Go ask Karen Thomas if she likes snakes and other icky critters. Maybe she won't mind getting married to a man who lets his children pick out his wife."

Mitch's face turned red with rage. How could she think such a thing? He reached for her shoulder. "Now, Hillary . . ."

She flinched at his touch and ran from the lab. She couldn't take anymore. Blinded by tears, she flung open the car door and climbed in. She used her coat sleeve to clear her eyes as she started the car.

Mitch watched her car back out of his driveway and kicked the side of the garage in frustration. Women! Go figure. He raised his fist toward the heavens and yelled, "Who in the hell is Karen Thomas?"

Ten

Mitch stared at the twinkling Christmas tree. From where he was sitting he counted twenty-five blue, eighteen red, twenty-eight green, and sixteen white blinking lights. The empty crystal punch bowl reflected the rainbow of flashing colors. Eunice must have gone especially light on the rum this year, because he was still sober and thinking clearly. Piles of brightly wrapped presents were stacked beneath the tree waiting for excited children to rip into them. He was afraid they might go unopened. His children had their hearts set on only one present, Hillary, and she wasn't under the tree.

Yesterday, after Hillary left, he had sat his children down for a lengthy talk. He had been stunned to hear their version of how he was marrying Hillary because of them. He could now understand why Hillary had been upset, but she should have believed in him and his love. Ethan had answered one important question though. Karen Thomas was the town's librarian, whom he'd never met, and their number-two choice for a mother. Hillary must have loved that piece of information.

After putting the kids to bed, he had gone over to her house only to find she wasn't there. He had dialed her number a couple of times; each time he got the annoying answering machine. She either wasn't picking up or had left town.

Tonight he had run over to her house three times. She hadn't been home. Callie had started to cry when it was bedtime and Hillary hadn't shown up yet. Eunice had glared at him, as though it were all his fault, and Ronnie made up some story about how Hillary had to go visit her parents on Christmas Eve. Ethan had still been optimistic that she would be there by morning.

Mitch absently stroked the white kitten curled up in his lap as the grandfather clock struck twelve. It was now officially Christmas Day. The kitten stretched and licked his finger. Hillary's Christmas present had shed all over his black pants, but he couldn't bring himself to put her down. The six-week-old feline had been the only bright spot in his evening. She had won the hearts of the children with her playful antics.

He placed the kitten in the wicker basket he had bought and turned out the lights. He slowly made his way to bed, then stared up at the ceiling for ten minutes before reaching for the phone on the nightstand and dialing Hillary's number. At the sound of the high-pitched beep he whispered, "Merry Christmas, love," and hung up.

* * *

Hillary looked away from the dark street she had been watching for the past hour. A light snow had just begun to fall. "No, Mom, I don't want to go with you and Dad to midnight mass." She mustered a sick-looking smile. "Thanks for asking, though."

Her mother and father exchanged concerned looks as they pulled on their coats. "Are you sure, dear?"

"Positive." She turned back to the window. "Drive carefully. It looks like the snow is finally sticking."

Her parents opened the door, allowing a wintery blast of freezing air in. "We'll see you when we get back."

Hillary watched as her parents' car backed out of the driveway and drove down the street. The faint outline of tire tracks were already being covered with more flakes. Didn't it snow in the movie *The Wizard of Oz*? Something about poppies. Hillary glanced at a streetlight to see how fast it was coming down. That's right, the good witch made it snow to wake Dorothy and the Cowardly Lion so they could continue their journey to the Emerald City.

Maybe that was what she needed. To be wakened. Hillary sat up straighter on the window seat, wondering if it had started to snow at Mitch's yet. Was he staring out a window, too, missing her as much as she was missing him?

For the past two days she had been going over it and over it. Mitch wasn't marrying her to please his children or anyone else. He had asked her to become his wife because he loved her. All she had to do was look into his eyes. It was there for all the world to see, and she had ignored it. She had allowed the past to cloud the future.

She was the cowardly lion. She was afraid to trust her instincts and her heart. They had failed her with Bruce, and she had run. She had run so hard that she left her job, her apartment, and even the city. When the scandal with the congressman happened, she hadn't physically run, but she'd hidden. She had allowed Mitch to straighten out the mess. It should have been she who demanded an apology, not Mitch. At the first hint of trouble in her relationship with Mitch, she had run to one of the few safe harbors left in her life, her parents' home. The house she had grown up in.

Hillary shuddered and wrapped her arms around her waist. She didn't like what she had become. It was definitely time for the lion to wake up and take charge of her life again.

When the children had dropped their bombshell on her, she should have sat down with Mitch to figure out what was going on. Instead, she'd allowed the .56 percent of doubt to transform the bombshell into an iceberg. She never gave Mitch a chance to respond to the charges. She had snapped out, tucked her tail between her legs, and run. She couldn't begin to imagine what he must be thinking of her by now.

The street was now covered with a white blanket. She quickly got up and packed her things. She had to get back to Mitch before the weather got worse. Her duffel bag was thrown in the backseat and her parents' Christmas present was placed under their tree with a hastily written note.

She was in love! She was 100 percent in love with Mitch. Not one flicker of doubt was left in her mind. She wanted to say those three special words to him, *"I love you."* She wanted to wish him a merry Christmas and snuggle into his warmth. She wanted to apologize for ever doubting his love. If it took her the rest of her life, she was going to make it up to him somehow.

She slammed the house door behind her and nearly danced down the driveway to her car. With the abandonment of a child, she looked up at the sky, opened her mouth, and stuck out her tongue. Plump moist snowflakes melted on her tongue. Maybe there were such things as good witches. The snow had wakened two cowardly lions. Hillary twirled in a circle and shouted "Thank you" to the cloud-heavy skies before getting in her car and heading for Oz.

Hillary circled Mitch's house and decided her first choice had been the correct one. The old paint-encrusted window in the living room was the one. It could be easily jimmied.

She trudged through the snow back to her car and started to unload the presents. What would Christmas morning be if her presents to everyone weren't under the tree? She carried the first load to the window and carefully set them down on the wooden porch that ran the entire length of the house.

After three trips the trunk was empty. The only present left was sitting in the passenger seat. Hillary chuckled as she unfastened the seat belt holding the six-foot lion in place. The Cowardly Lion Toy Emporium had just lost its mascot. The sweet elderly couple who owned and ran the shop had made a fatal mistake when they handed Hillary a business card the day she purchased the expensive train set and half a dozen houses for Ethan. Their names had been on the card. A quick check in the telephone directory had given Hillary their home address. They had just gotten home from Christmas Eve church services when she arrived on their doorstep begging them to open the shop so she could buy the lion.

The sweet couple couldn't resist the heart-wrenching story she had spilled about a misunderstanding and how she needed the lion to show Mitch how much she loved him. They hadn't understood how a lion would help, but then again, they still hadn't gotten over a marriage proposal that read SURRENDER HILLARY. Within fifteen minutes the shop was open, her credit card was sizzling, and her furry friend was enjoying a ride through town. She had promised the couple invitations to the wedding, which she pledged to be a normal affair. Though the couple had chuckled disbelievingly, they accepted the invitation. They wouldn't miss it for the world.

Hillary struggled through the falling snow, trying not to drag her heavy buddy on the wet ground. She had to stop halfway to the house to rest against a huge maple. Her coat was damp with melted flakes, and her wild hair had more fizz than Alka-Seltzer. She picked the lion's snow-covered tail off the ground. "What did they stuff you with? Bricks?"

Her buddy remained silent.

She wrapped her arms under the lion and half dragged, half carried him onto the porch. She slumped against the house and caught her breath. She had made it!

From her vantage point she looked out over the neighborhood. Most of the houses had their Christmas lights still lit. Shining plastic Santas riding in plastic sleighs decorated several roof-tops. The white blanket of snow set everything off to perfection. It was a picture-perfect Christmas Eve—correction, make that a picture-perfect Christmas. It was way after midnight, and all good little boys and girls should be tucked in their beds, dreaming of sugarplums. She hoped Mitch was tucked into his, because that's where she was going to deliver his present.

Hillary dug in her wallet and pulled out a credit card. It took her three attempts before the card unlatched the old lock on the window. She held the card up and kissed it. "It's a good thing I never leave home without you," she said, then replaced it in her purse.

Five minutes later Hillary had exhausted every curse word she knew. The window wouldn't budge. Eunice must have painted it shut. It was either ring the doorbell and wake the entire house or attempt to force the window and pray everyone inside were all heavy sleepers. Using the palm of her hand, she gave the window frame a couple of whacks. The window started to give. Encouraged, she banged on it a couple of more times until she was sure it would go up.

She waited. No lights in the house went on. No one had heard the commotion. She slowly raised the waist-high window and glanced into the room. The faint outlines of the couch and Christmas tree were all she needed to know that Eunice hadn't repainted or moved the furniture in the past two days.

Mitch had held his breath as the window was raised. His house was being burglarized! He saw someone's head stick in and glance around. Whoever the perpetrator was had to be the worst burglar in history. Granted, Mitch hadn't been asleep when he heard the banging going on downstairs, but it had been loud enough to wake the dead. Two sleepless nights had taken their toll. Whoever this joker was, he was going to be sorry he had picked Mitch's house to rob.

Ethan and Callie slowly made their way down the dark stairs and hid behind a chair. Santa had come! Both had heard all the noise downstairs and knew the big man himself had arrived. Their eyes opened wider as the window was raised. Whatever happened to using the chimney?

Eunice quietly made her way from her bedroom through the kitchen. She picked up the largest frying pan she could find and continued toward the living room, where all the racket had been coming from. When the noise had first woken her up, she thought it had been the kitten getting into some mischief. But when the banging persisted, she figured it was either a burglar or the ghost of Jacob Marley paying a visit. She lifted the pan higher and prayed it was a burglar. Crooks she could handle; she wasn't too sure about ghosts.

Ronnie jammed the cartridge into the .38 Special and released the safety. She hoped the noise was either Eunice hanging pictures at one in the morning, or the oil burner knocking like crazy. Her instincts told her differently though. They shouted, "Intruder!" Ronnie silently opened her attic bedroom door and slipped down to the second-floor landing. She was standing in the blackness at the top of the stairs staring down into the living room when the window was raised. Her instincts had been right again.

Hillary looked at the pile of presents sitting on the porch and sighed. Just the thought of climbing in and out of the window until all the gifts were in was tiring. She had already built up a sweat lugging a seventy-pound lion across the yard. She might as well take the heaviest in first and be done with it. Hillary turned to the lion and hoisted him up onto the windowsill.

Mitch saw the large frame of the thief start to come through the window. Lord, he was a bigger man than he had anticipated. It was too late now to find a weapon to defend himself with. Not knowing what he was about to face, he decided the element of surprise was his best defense. Mitch lunged himself at the burglar and wrestled him to the carpet.

The coffee table was knocked over and presents were scattered in the melee. Mitch grunted as he rolled across the rug, taking the crook with him. With a hoarse shout of victory Mitch pinned the thief to the carpet.

Ronnie saw her brother tackle the burglar, but in the dark room she couldn't make out who was winning. All she could perceive was a mass of arms and legs rolling around under the tree. She dashed down the steps and took the official stance. With her knees bent and a two-handed grip on the gun, she shouted, "Police, freeze!"

Eunice had seen Mitch attack the intruder. Not knowing who was getting the upper hand, she shouted her encouragements: "Get him, Mitch!" She ran over to the light switch. "Smash him a good one!" With a flick of her hand she raised every switch on the wall.

Both living-room lights went on, the tree lit up, and a chorus of "Deck the Halls" blared in the room. All eyes turned to the man Mitch was straddling.

Mitch glanced down into the timid expression of

a lion's face. He had wrestled with a stuffed animal!

Ronnie raised her gun and flipped on the safety. She bit her lip to keep from laughing out loud. Eunice lowered the pan and chuckled. Ethan and Callie's huge eyes never blinked as they took in the sight before them.

Soft musical laughter floated into the room from the window.

Hillary sat on the windowsill and laughed. The scene that greeted her was priceless. It would never make the front of a Christmas greeting card.

Mitch was sitting on top of the lion. His arm was back, ready to deliver a stunning blow in case the critter moved. He was wearing the pair of boxer shorts she had given him last week—the red ones printed with cows kissing under branches of mistletoe. A strand of silver tinsel clung to his bare back, and one was dangling from his hair. He looked ridiculous and sexy.

Eunice was standing by the light switch wearing a robe that, years ago, should have been used as a rag to clean paintbrushes with. Her hair was up in huge fluorescent-green rollers that were twisted in every direction and big, floppy duck slippers graced her feet. At least she thought they were ducks. They were furry and yellow, and huge orange bills were sticking out of them. Hillary would bet the balance due on her credit card that Mitch had bought them for her. The heavy frying pan she was holding looked lethal.

Ronnie looked like a pinup girl for *Police Quarterly*. Her hair held that just-out-of-bed look, and the PAL T-shirt she had been sleeping in barely covered the essentials. Her unyielding position and the deadly gleam of her gun would have caused any thief to surrender.

Ethan and Callie were staring over the back of a wing chair, their eyes looking as though they were ready to pop out of their sockets.

Hillary loved them all dearly. She wouldn't trade Mitch or his feisty family for anything in the world. They had all come prepared to fight what they thought was a burglar. Bravery obviously was a family trait. She slipped off the windowsill and into the room. "Ho, ho, ho. Merry Christmas."

Mitch found his voice the same instant his children did. "Hillary!" they shouted in unison.

She bent down and picked up the big red satin bow that had been knocked off the lion. How was she going to explain to her ex-fiancé why she was breaking into his house? "If you don't like your Christmas present, just say so, Mitch. You don't have to beat it up."

Mitch glanced back down at the six-foot lion. "He's for me?"

"Seems to me that you fell in love with a coward. . . . She isn't one any longer, and I wanted you to have a reminder of the old me."

Mitch slowly stood up and shook his head. "You were never a coward."

"Yes, I was." She glanced at the others in the room. She had wished she and Mitch could have been alone for this conversation, but it wasn't necessary. She had courage now. "Every time things got tough in my life, I ran. I allowed mistakes from my past to guide my future." With tears shining in her eyes, she said, "I'm not running anymore."

Mitch crossed the space that separated them in three steps, then hauled her into his arm and kissed her. Hillary was back!

Eunice and Ronnie smiled knowingly at each other and tried to usher the children out of the room.

"Look! Santa came!" Callie cried out. She had spotted a purple bike near the tree. It had a big red bow and a tag printed with her name. "It's just like the one that's in Gerhart's store window." She ran across the room and hopped on it. The bike was a perfect fit.

Ethan tore across the room toward the stacks of presents under the tree. He picked up the first one bearing his name and began to tear off the paper. Red wrapping paper, printed with little snowmen, went sailing across the room.

Eunice and Ronnie looked at each other and shrugged their shoulders. They had tried to give Mitch and Hillary some privacy, but nothing short of an earthquake could have stopped the kids from opening their presents. In a silent mutual agreement they left the living room and headed back to bed.

Ethan's cry of pleasure split the air. He held up the box containing the remote-controlled airplane he had always wanted. "Look, Callie!"

Mitch reluctantly broke the kiss and wrapped his arm around Hillary's shoulder. Her coat was damp and cold against his bare chest, but he wasn't letting her go. She felt too wonderful.

He gazed at his children and smiled. Their

young faces shone with the joy and wonder of Christmas morning. Mitch didn't have the heart to send the kids back to bed now. He and Hillary would just have to wait until all the presents were opened. He didn't mind. He'd already gotten his Christmas wish—Hillary. "What made you come here tonight?"

Hillary watched as Ethan tore into another package. To think she'd almost missed this. Her arm around Mitch's waist squeezed. "The snow."

"Snow?" Mitch looked out the opened window. Sure enough, it was snowing. He shivered and closed the window while Hillary took off her coat.

Ethan and Callie dashed over and pressed their noses to the pane of glass. They stared in wonder at the white flakes coming down. Nothing delighted or captured a child's imagination more than the first snowfall of the season.

"Can we go sledding?" Ethan asked.

"Can we build a snowman?" Callie asked.

Mitch chuckled. "We'll see tomorrow morning."

"Hey, you two," Hillary said, "doesn't your Christmas present deserve a hug?" She bent down, held out her arms, and waited.

Ethan and Callie looked at each other and grinned. In a flash they flew into Hillary's opened arms.

Her eyes filled with tears as she hugged the children tightly. She glanced up at Mitch and gave him a smile. Was it possible to love someone more than 100 percent?

Ethan and Callie squeezed her back. They had gotten their wish. They had gotten a mother for Christmas. When Hillary released them, they stepped back and grinned up at their father. "Thanks, Dad."

"You're welcome." Mitch hauled Hillary back into his arms and kissed her.

Ethan looked at his father and new mother and then at the stack of presents still under the tree. He pulled Callie aside and whispered something. Callie wistfully stared at the presents but nodded in agreement.

"Dad, we're tired," Ethan said. "We're going back to bed now." Ethan grabbed Callie's hand and yanked her toward the stairs. "Good night."

Mitch knew what this must be costing them. He vowed to make it up to them somehow. "All right. I'm sure I'll be seeing you both bright and early in the morning though."

"Yeah." Ethan started up the steps with his sister in tow.

Callie stopped halfway up the steps, turned, and looked at her dad. "Can we get the baby brother for next Christmas?"

Mitch started to choke, and Hillary laughed. "We'll talk about that later, okay, sweetheart?"

Callie looked at Hillary and grinned. "Okay, Mom."

Hillary felt the tears start to build again as the kids disappeared up the steps.

Mitch pulled her back into his arms. He was standing in a freezing-cold room with only his underwear on, but he had never felt warmer in his life. "What was that about a baby brother?"

"I'll explain it to you later—right now I have another present for you."

He gazed down into her smiling face. "I'll get it later, right now all I want to do is hold you."

"You don't have to release me to get it."

Mitch grinned. "I like the sound of this."

She reached up and tenderly ran a finger down his whisker-roughened cheek. "I love you."

His heart leaped in his chest. She had just given him the best Christmas present of all. "I think I've waited a lifetime for you to say those words." He bent and captured her mouth in a tender kiss. "I love you too."

"Mitch?"

His lips were teasing the sensitive spot behind her ear, the spot that, when nuzzled, made her knees go weak. "Hmmm . . ."

"Does your bedroom door have a lock on it?"

He quickly raised his head. "Yes, why?"

"Because I have another present I want to give to you." She smiled invitingly.

"Lord, I can't wait to unwrap it." Mitch picked her up and started to carry her from the room. A small meowing sound coming from under the couch stopped him before he could turn out the lights. In all the noise and excitement he had forgotten about the kitten.

Hillary glanced over his shoulder to see what the noise was. She screamed in delight as a small bundle of white fur crawled out. "Look, a kitten!"

Mitch lowered Hillary to her feet and picked up the ball of fur. He carefully handed it to Hillary. "Merry Christmas, love. Your first pet."

"He's mine?" She cuddled the kitten against her cheek.

"It's a she, and yes, she's all yours." Mitch smiled at the way she was bravely holding back the tears. "What are you going to name her?"

Hillary looked at the kitten and then back at Mitch. "Snow. I think I'll name her Snow."

THE EDITOR'S CORNER

Next month LOVESWEPT salutes **MEN IN UNIFORM**, those daring heroes who risk all for life, liberty . . . and the pursuit of women they desire. **MEN IN UNIFORM** are experts at plotting seductive maneuvers, and in six fabulous romances, you'll be at the front lines of passion as each of these men wages a battle for the heart of the woman he loves.

The first of our dashing heroes is Brett Upton in **JUST FRIENDS** by Laura Taylor, LOVESWEPT #600—and he's furious about the attack on Leah Holbrook's life, the attack that cost her her memory and made her forget the love they'd once shared and that he'd betrayed. Now, as he desperately guards her, he dares to believe that fate has given him a second chance to win back the only woman he's ever wanted. Laura will hold you spellbound with this powerful romance.

In **FLYBOY** by Victoria Leigh, LOVESWEPT #601, veteran Air Force pilot Matt Cooper has seen plenty of excitement, but nothing compares to the storm of desire he feels when he rescues Jennifer Delaney from a raging typhoon. Matt has always called the world his home, but the redhead suddenly makes him long to settle down. And with wildfire embraces and whispers of passionate fantasies, he sets out to make the independent beauty share his newfound dream. A splendid love story, told with plenty of Victoria's wit.

Patricia Potter returns to LOVESWEPT with **TROUBA-DOUR**, LOVESWEPT #602. Connor MacLaren is fiercely masculine in a kilt—and from the moment she first lays eyes on him, Leslie Turner feels distinctly overwhelmed. Hired as a publicist for the touring folk-singer, she'd expected anything except this rugged Scot who awakens a reckless hunger she'd never dare confess. But armed with a killer grin and potent kisses, Connor vows to make her surrender to desire. You'll treasure this enchanting romance from Pat.

In her new LOVESWEPT, **HART'S LAW,** #603, Theresa Gladden gives us a sexy sheriff whose smile can melt steel. When Johnny Hart hears that Bailey Asher's coming home, he remembers kissing her breathless the summer she was seventeen—and wonders if she'd still feel so good in his embrace. But Bailey no longer trusts men and she insists on keeping her distance. How Johnny convinces her to open her arms—and heart—to him once more makes for one of Theresa's best LOVESWEPTs.

SURRENDER, BABY, LOVESWEPT #604 by Suzanne Forster, is Geoff Dias's urgent message to Miranda Witherspoon. A soldier of fortune, Geoff has seen and done it all, but nothing burns in his memory more than that one night ten years ago when he'd tasted fierce passion in Miranda's arms. When he agrees to help her find her missing fiancé, he has just one objective in mind: to make her see they're destined only for each other. The way Suzanne writes, the sexual sparks practically leap off the page!

Finally, in **HEALING TOUCH** by Judy Gill, LOVESWEPT #605, army doctor Rob McGee needs a wife to help him raise his young orphaned niece—but what he wants is

Heather Tomasi! He met the lovely temptress only once two years before, but his body still remembers the silk of her skin and the wicked promises in her eyes. She's definitely not marriage material, but Rob has made up his mind. And he'll do anything—even bungee jump—to prove to her that he's the man she needs. Judy will delight you with this wonderful tale.

On sale this month from FANFARE are four fabulous novels. From highly acclaimed author Deborah Smith comes **BLUE WILLOW,** a gloriously heart-stopping love story with characters as passionate and bold as the South that brought them forth. Artemas Colebrook and Lily MacKenzie are bound to each other through the Blue Willow estate . . . and by a passion that could destroy all they have struggled for.

The superstar of the sensual historical, Susan Johnson tempts you with **SINFUL.** Set in the 1780s, Chelsea Ferguson must escape a horrible fate—marriage to a man she doesn't love—by bedding another man. But Sinjin St. John, Duke of Seth, refuses to be her rescuer and Chelsea must resort to a desperate deception that turns into a passionate adventure.

Bestselling LOVESWEPT author Helen Mittermeyer has penned **THE PRINCESS OF THE VEIL,** a breathtakingly romantic tale set in long-ago Scotland and Iceland. When Viking princess Iona is captured by the notorious Scottish chief Magnus Sinclair, she vows never to belong to him, though he would make her his bride.

Theresa Weir, author of the widely praised **FOREVER,** delivers a new novel of passion and drama. In **LAST SUMMER,** movie star Johnnie Irish returns to his Texas hometown, intent on getting revenge. But all thoughts of getting even disappear when he meets the beautiful widow Maggie Mayfield.

Also on sale this month in the hardcover edition from Doubleday is **SACRED LIES** by Dianne Edouard and Sandra Ware. In this sexy contemporary novel, Romany Chase must penetrate the inner sanctum of the Vatican on a dangerous mission . . . and walk a fine line between two men who could be friend or foe.

Happy reading!

With warmest wishes,

Nita Taublib

Nita Taublib
Associate Publisher
LOVESWEPT and FANFARE

OFFICIAL RULES TO WINNERS CLASSIC SWEEPSTAKES

No Purchase necessary. To enter the sweepstakes follow instructions found elsewhere in this offer. You can also enter the sweepstakes by hand printing your name, address, city, state and zip code on a 3" x 5" piece of paper and mailing it to: Winners Classic Sweepstakes, P.O. Box 785, Gibbstown, NJ 08027. Mail each entry separately. Sweepstakes begins 12/1/91. Entries must be received by 6/1/93. Some presentations of this sweepstakes may feature a deadline for the Early Bird prize. If the offer you receive does, then to be eligible for the Early Bird prize your entry must be received according to the Early Bird date specified. Not responsible for lost, late, damaged, misdirected, illegible or postage due mail. Mechanically reproduced entries are not eligible. All entries become property of the sponsor and will not be returned.

Prize Selection/Validations: Winners will be selected in random drawings on or about 7/30/93, by VENTURA ASSOCIATES, INC., an independent judging organization whose decisions are final. Odds of winning are determined by total number of entries received. Circulation of this sweepstakes is estimated not to exceed 200 million. Entrants need not be present to win. All prizes are guaranteed to be awarded and delivered to winners. Winners will be notified by mail and may be required to complete an affidavit of eligibility and release of liability which must be returned within 14 days of date of notification or alternate winners will be selected. Any guest of a trip winner will also be required to execute a release of liability. Any prize notification letter or any prize returned to a participating sponsor, Bantam Doubleday Dell Publishing Group, Inc., its participating divisions or subsidiaries, or VENTURA ASSOCIATES, INC. as undeliverable will be awarded to an alternate winner. Prizes are not transferable. No multiple prize winners except as may be necessary due to unavailability, in which case a prize of equal or greater value will be awarded. Prizes will be awarded approximately 90 days after the drawing. All taxes, automobile license and registration fees, if applicable, are the sole responsibility of the winners. Entry constitutes permission (except where prohibited) to use winners' names and likenesses for publicity purposes without further or other compensation.

Participation: This sweepstakes is open to residents of the United States and Canada, except for the province of Quebec. This sweepstakes is sponsored by Bantam Doubleday Dell Publishing Group, Inc. (BDD), 666 Fifth Avenue, New York, NY 10103. Versions of this sweepstakes with different graphics will be offered in conjunction with various solicitations or promotions by different subsidiaries and divisions of BDD. Employees and their families of BDD, its division, subsidiaries, advertising agencies, and VENTURA ASSOCIATES, INC., are not eligible.

Canadian residents, in order to win, must first correctly answer a time limited arithmetical skill testing question. Void in Quebec and wherever prohibited or restricted by law. Subject to all federal, state, local and provincial laws and regulations.

Prizes: The following values for prizes are determined by the manufacturers' suggested retail prices or by what these items are currently known to be selling for at the time this offer was published. Approximate retail values include handling and delivery of prizes. Estimated maximum retail value of prizes: 1 Grand Prize ($27,500 if merchandise or $25,000 Cash); 1 First Prize ($3,000); 5 Second Prizes ($400 each); 35 Third Prizes ($100 each); 1,000 Fourth Prizes ($9.00 each) ; 1 Early Bird Prize ($5,000); Total approximate maximum retail value is $50,000. Winners will have the option of selecting any prize offered at level won. Automobile winner must have a valid driver's license at the time the car is awarded. Trips are subject to space and departure availability. Certain black-out dates may apply. Travel must be completed within one year from the time the prize is awarded. Minors must be accompanied by an adult. Prizes won by minors will be awarded in the name of parent or legal guardian.

For a list of Major Prize Winners (available after 7/30/93): send a self-addressed, stamped envelope entirely separate from your entry to: Winners Classic Sweepstakes Winners, P.O. Box 825, Gibbstown, NJ 08027. Requests must be received by 6/1/93. DO NOT SEND ANY OTHER CORRESPONDENCE TO THIS P.O. BOX.

Women's Fiction

On Sale in February

TEMPERATURES RISING
56054-X $5.99/6.99 in Canada
☐
by Sandra Brown
New York Times bestselling author of
A WHOLE NEW LIGHT and FRENCH SILK
A contemporary tale of love and passion in the South Pacific

OUTLAW HEARTS
29807-0 $5.50/6.50 in Canada
☐
by Rosanne Bittner
Bestselling author of SONG OF THE WOLF,
praised by *Romantic Times* as "a stunning
achievement...that moves the soul and fills the heart."

THE LAST HIGHWAYMAN
56065-4 $5.50/6.50 in Canada
☐
by Katherine O'Neal
Fascinating historical fact and sizzling romantic fiction meet
in this sensual tale of a legendary bandit and a scandalous
high-born lady.

CONFIDENCES
56170-7 $4.99/5.99 in Canada
☐
by Penny Hayden
"Thirtysomething" meets Danielle Steel—four best friends
are bound by an explosive secret.

Ask for these books at your local bookstore or use this page to order.

☐ Please send me the books I have checked above. I am enclosing $ _____ (add $2.50 to cover postage and handling). Send check or money order, no cash or C. O. D.'s please.

Name _____

Address _____

City/ State/ Zip _____

Send order to: Bantam Books, Dept. FN94, 2451 S. Wolf Rd., Des Plaines, IL 60018
Allow four to six weeks for delivery.

Prices and availability subject to change without notice.

FN94 2/93

FANFARE

Bestselling Women's Fiction

Sandra Brown

_____	29783-X A WHOLE NEW LIGHT	$5.99/6.99 in Canada
_____	29500-4 TEXAS! SAGE	$4.99/5.99
_____	29085-1 22 INDIGO PLACE	$4.50/5.50
_____	28990-X TEXAS! CHASE	$4.99/5.99
_____	28951-9 TEXAS! LUCKY	$4.99/5.99

Amanda Quick

_____	29325-7 RENDEZVOUS	$4.99/5.99
_____	28354-5 SEDUCTION	$4.99/5.99
_____	28932-2 SCANDAL	$4.95/5.95
_____	28594-7 SURRENDER..	$4.50/5.50

Nora Roberts

_____	29597-7 CARNAL INNOCENCE	$5.50/6.50
_____	29078-9 GENUINE LIES......................................	$4.99/5.99
_____	28578-5 PUBLIC SECRETS	$4.95/5.95
_____	26461-3 HOT ICE	$4.99/5.99
_____	26574-1 SACRED SINS	$5.50/6.50
_____	27859-2 SWEET REVENGE	$5.50/6.50
_____	27283-7 BRAZEN VIRTUE	$4.99/5.99

Iris Johansen

_____	29871-2 LAST BRIDGE HOME	$4.50/5.50
_____	29604-3 THE GOLDEN BARBARIAN	$4.99/5.99
_____	29244-7 REAP THE WIND	$4.99/5.99
_____	29032-0 STORM WINDS	$4.99/5.99
_____	28855-5 THE WIND DANCER.............................	$4.95/5.95

Ask for these titles at your bookstore or use this page to order.

Please send me the books I have checked above. I am enclosing $ _____ (add $2.50 to cover postage and handling). Send check or money order, no cash or C. O. D.'s please.

Mr./ Ms. _____

Address _____

City/ State/ Zip _____

Send order to: Bantam Books, Dept. FN 16, 2451 S. Wolf Road, Des Plaines, IL 60018

Please allow four to six weeks for delivery.

Prices and availability subject to change without notice.   FN 16 - 8/92